Kai's Heart

Karst Series
Book One

Renee MacKenzie

Kai's Heart

Karst Series
Book One

Renee MacKenzie

Affinity Rainbow Publications

2018

ACKNOWLEDGMENTS

I would like to thank the Affinity Rainbow Publications team—JM Dragon, Erin O'Reilly, and Nancy Kaufman—for continuing to support my writing. Thank you to Angela Koenig for the magnificent editing and Alexis Smith for proof editing. I want to send a shout out to so many of the other Affinity writers who are now truly like sisters to me. I raise my glass (of Fireball, of course) to you all.

Many, many thanks to my first readers—Christine Clark, Kit Carrington, and Sandi Baum—your insights and suggestions were amazing.

Kai Brodie came to me in a rush of words, images, and keen emotions when I least expected it. And then Samantha Brodek brought her to life in the image incorporated into the cover art. Thank you Samantha for sharing your immense artistic talent with me, Kai, and the world.

Finally, a resounding thank you to the readers. Without the readers there would be no *Kai's Heart*.

DEDICATION

For Pam, always

TABLE OF CONTENTS

PROLOGUE

The sun is bright on this clear day. I pull my eye shades from the pocket of my denim cargo pants and place them on my face, letting them block the strongest rays. The low rumble of a distant generator is barely discernible. A lone coywolf in the distance yowls, a plaintive sound that makes me wonder why the animal is not resting in the shade.

I stand on an unnamed ridge southeast of Grover, staring down at ND3—National Detention #3—which is believed to be the most brutal of the five detention centers used by the Anointed to imprison us Resisters. I don't know if what I hear is true, if the place is as dangerous as is speculated. That is all it is, speculation, as no one has made it out alive to describe it—not since the Anointed have taken over. The few stories I have heard don't disturb me as much as the ones I have not.

There is a man living at my family's homestead who says he escaped from an Employment Center. The ECs are really just slave labor facilities, but at least the people live in an internment camp, not a prison like the detention centers. I keep my distance from this man, not liking the way he looks at me.

The eye shades help, but I still blink against the bright sun. I pull off my wide-brimmed hat to adjust the bun that my hair is pulled tightly into.

I scan the vastness before me. If I don't look to the north where the land is scorched, the view is breathtaking. The sunlight blinks off a patch of solar panels, used for ND3, and I reflect for a moment on the stories I've heard about New America before the power was restored. No time for negative thoughts, though.

The sky is the bluest blue but a wind can move in with no warning and fill it with clouds darkened by dust and debris. With the heavy rains likely months away, there is no real hope for relief from the dry, crackling heat.

Even with its unrelenting weather, New America is a magnificent country, despite its being governed by the Anointed tyrants.

Living in a hidden homestead in an unfriendly landscape and hiding from the enemy soldiers is all that I know. My entire twenty-two years of life on this post-World War III earth have been spent training for—and anticipating—the Revolution.

The note in my denim's pocket indicates that the time is growing near. Today my mission is to deliver the note to the Resistance Army's second in command, the aging General Eli Grayson.

I must get moving.

PART ONE—INMATE 8895

CHAPTER ONE

I stumble into the wall of the processing room when the guard shoves me forward. My bare hip scrapes the dirty surface of the cement block wall. A heavy metal door crashes shut. Once alone, I run my hands over the stubble on my newly shorn head. I don't have to touch my neck where the guard grabbed me earlier to know the area will be tender where his fingers have most likely left their mark.

I am vulnerable and exposed without my clothing, but I try to steady my breathing. My throat is raw from dry-swallowing the note I had to hide from my captors. At least it didn't end up in the wrong hands, I tell myself as consolation.

I've not handled things well so far. I was so unafraid of being caught, so complacent after a lifetime living on the outside, that when the soldiers approached me near the city of Grover, I was unprepared. They had asked over and over where I'd come from and where I was going. I'd known immediately that things wouldn't end well for me. Without any real options, I put on my best confused look. "Can you give me directions to Grover?"

The door opens and a shirt and pair of denims land at my feet.

"Get dressed."

I scramble to gather the clothing off the sticky floor.

"Hurry up. Or do you want another cavity search?"

Bile rises in my throat and I dress as quickly as I can. A murderous rage is building in me and I know I must tamp it down. I focus. Rule number one—always know your mission. Today my mission is to stay alive—hopefully with humanity and dignity, but those are not deal breakers.

The guard grabs me by the arm and yanks me toward him.

"Pagan mutant," he says, spittle hitting me.

I want to punch him in his pale face so badly it sickens me. If I had my prized knife, the one they all but drooled over when they confiscated it from me, I would bury it in his chest, all the way to the hilt.

The guards had eyed me suspiciously as I was processed in, but not nearly as critically as the other prisoners are doing now as I make my way down the long corridor. My fellow Resisters will want to know how I managed to survive on the outside without proper documentation. People just didn't come in new to the system anymore. Only Resistance prisoners who'd been kicked out of one of the Employment Camps came in to any detention center now, or an Anointed, one who'd broken the law, especially if that law was against the Bible or helping a Resister.

I am afraid I will see recognition on the faces of the other prisoners, but then I decide the gaunt, slack faces around me belong to women who've been incarcerated since before I was even born. The thought offers relief, then floods me with despair.

I hear the mutterings from the other prisoners.

"She must be a spy. She's an Anointed pretending to be a Resister."

"No," someone else chimes in. "She's from the North territory, spying for them."

"No one comes or goes from the North!"

The mention of the North territories gets my attention. It is on the other side of the scorched, black wasteland protected by unstable canyons and craters. Rumor has it that this strip of northern land is a bastion of peace, but I don't know anyone who has ever been there and come back to tell about it.

Before long, even the guards are whispering about me.

"She's here to check up on us."

"No, she's here to bring word from the family members at the ECs or other NDs."

"Or maybe she's just a dimwitted pagan who's been stumbling around on the outside all this time, getting away with it out of pure, dumb luck." A guard laughs. "Not that we could tell that by looking at her. All those pagans look like they have damaged DNA."

I ignore the laughter that ensues. I hold my head high because the Anointed may have conquered my people over two decades ago, but soon the Resistance Revolution Army will turn the tide and I will be free again. I just have to survive until then.

"Go on, move it." The guard nudges me forward.

Some of the prisoners are lingering in the open doorways to the cells with the large, barred doors, while others mill about the corridor. I will learn soon enough how much time outside the cells we get.

I walk until I am shoved into the entrance to a cell and glance around what will presumably be my home away from home. There is one window, boarded up from the outside except for the top two or three inches. There are two sets of bunk beds, of which three beds look obviously claimed. The last, a bottom bunk, has no sheets or pillow, just a soiled, inch-thick mattress. I sit on the edge of that bunk.

"Did I tell you to sit, inmate?"

I jump up, instinctively, but when I see the woman is dressed as I am in denims and work shirt, with her head shorn close to the scalp, I know she is just another prisoner. I sit back down.

"Seriously?" the woman asks. "Did you seriously just show me disrespect?"

I don't answer, instead I mentally prepare myself to fight if the other woman doesn't back down. I glance at the door to the cell. Two other women—one black and one Hispanic—stand in the doorway, arms crossed over their chests. The lighter of the two laughs until the other elbows her roughly.

I pivot around on the mattress and stretch out my legs. I mean to show that I am relaxed, but every fiber of me is ready to defend myself.

"All right then," the woman says. She pushes my legs to the side, but before I can strike at her, she sits on the edge of the mattress. "We have some rules."

The others come in to stand by the bunk.

I raise an eyebrow, but do not speak.

"First, we mind our own business, but have each other's back. That means don't bring any drama or dirty skanks into our little slice of real estate." The woman smiles. "Clean women are welcome, but not dirty skanks. You get my drift?"

"Yeah," I lie. "Whatever." I nudge her with my leg, and the woman gets up. I sit up.

"What's your name?" the first woman asks.

I look at her. She is a similar amalgam of features as I am, making her ancestry almost impossible to guess. "I am Inmate 8895."

The woman who had sat next to me shakes her head. "I'm Bea. This is Maria and Terry."

I nod with a slight bow to each.

"Where are you from?" Bea asks.

"Nowhere, and everywhere."

"Where have you been if you aren't coming from a work farm?"

"How do you know I'm not coming from one?"

"Everyone knows you came from the outside, out of thin air, like a spy."

A shrill alarm sounds in the corridor.

"Evening head count," the woman named Terry explains. "We line up in the hall. After that we will be confined to our cells for the rest of the night."

At the other end of the hall a prisoner is being berated for having the audacity to look a guard in the eye. Note to self, no eye contact with the guards.

The two guards who walk slowly past are thumping pieces of metal piping against their legs as they do so. They wear dark green cargo pants and gray polo shirts. I work hard to train my focus over the right shoulder of each guard as they pause in front of me.

The women to both sides of me are holding out a cloth. I see the last guard squirt what appears to be tooth gel onto the cloth of the woman beside me. At the last second I extend my hand slightly and with only a moment of hesitation, the guard squirts some gel directly onto my fingers.

I wait until I am back at my bunk to scrub the gel onto my teeth. I need to figure out how to get one of those cloths. Maybe it will come with my bed sheets?

†

On my second day at ND3, I sit on my bunk; the only other person in the cell with me is Maria. I am bringing my mind to a quiet place, settling down the anger over being incarcerated, before I venture out again into the corridor that will lead me to a dayroom and cafeteria, as well as other places I've yet to imagine. A bell rings in a curious pattern.

"What's that?" I ask Maria.

"That's the shower call. Leave your boots here," Maria instructs. "If you leave them by the shower they'll be taken by some greedy guard."

I strip off my boots and follow my bunkmates down the corridor where we line up against a wall, moving slowly. The women ahead of me start to strip so I do as well. All of our clothing goes into a big bin.

The mold in the shower hangs in the air and clings to the walls, ceiling, and floor. We all shuffle in. My foot hits a slick spot and I think I'm going to fall, but the woman behind me grabs my arm.

"Easy," she whispers. I make eye contact for just a moment, memorizing her features to ensure I will know the face of this kind stranger later.

Rings hang in a row from the ceiling. The women hurry to grab the closest one to them. I grow panicked that it's some kind of lottery system; fewer rings than women and the women who don't get one get… what? Stoned? Trampled?

I grab a ring with one hand and leave the other arm draped self-consciously across my bare body. I glance around and all I can see are ribs and the sharp angles of hips on the emaciated women. I am thin, and always have been, but some of these women are only a ration or two away from starvation.

As soon as the water rushes from the hose at the other end of the shower, I grab the ring with my other hand. The water hits the women before me with such force that I fear it might knock me down when it comes to me.

In the back by the door, a guard stands with his legs parted and arms crossed over his chest as he watches the man with the offending hose. I've seen the man with the deep scar across his forehead a few times. He holds my gaze before making a show of squeezing his eyes shut and puffing out his cheeks as if holding his breath. I understand what he means just seconds before the water blasts at my face. I close my eyes and hold my breath with only a fraction of a second to spare. I will remember the scarred man's face—I will have mercy on him if I get my revenge on the others.

The cold water leaves me breathless for several seconds. Its force feels like being struck.

The blast of water is assaulting the woman to my right when I see a wrinkled, dark woman lose her hold on her overhead ring. She falls to the ground where the guard sprays her cruelly in her face. The guard with the hose turns off the water and marches over to the woman.

"What's your problem, inmate?"

I take a chance and glance around again at the other women. They are all so thin, I wonder if food is used as a reward in this place, and if it is, will I be able to comply.

The woman gets up onto her hands and knees just as the guard turns the hose back on and uses the water to knock her back down.

"Get up, inmate!" He kicks her several times before walking away from her. "You are being disruptive! Maybe you need some time in Isolation?"

I consider letting go of my ring to help the woman up when the water blasts back at me, hitting me knee-level and almost knocking my legs out from under me. I'm forced to hold onto the ring with all of my strength.

"Round two," the scarred guard in the back yells out.

Now the water hitting us has a stringent, disinfectant smell to it. I hold my breath for what feels like several long minutes as the sudsy water assaults me. Another woman falls and I keep my eyes closed until the scarred guard says, "Rinse."

"Cooper, you're taking the sport out of it for me."

"Come on, Powers, just finish so we can get on with our day."

I make a mental note: Cooper good, Powers bad. I am keeping score.

On the way out of the shower, a guard abruptly thrusts a bundle of clean clothing at each of us. No one looks at him directly as they take the offering and walk, naked, back to the bunks. I follow the woman in front of me until I peel off to my cell.

"Survived your first shower, I see," Bea says.

I don't respond because I am so angry that my bunkmates didn't see fit to clue me in about the process of the showers, and I don't wish to risk saying the wrong thing. I silently examine the shirt I've been given, then notice the small square of cloth I can use to scrub my teeth.

"It's always a crap shoot whether your clothes will fit or not. And it's easier to come back here and dry a little before you put them on." Maria holds up her pants. "I'll be wearing pants that are much too short unless I can find someone with longer ones who will trade with me."

"I'll trade you mine if you throw in some cigarettes," Bea says.

"I don't have any cigs." Maria opens the top of the pants as if ready to step in.

I examine my pants. They appear to be a few inches longer than hers, so I hold them out to Maria.

"Thank you," Maria says as she hands me hers.

"No problem." Why not, I muse, at least Maria had warned me not to wear my boots to the shower.

†

Two more days pass and I am contemplating my odds of survival as I linger in a corridor. I want to keep my head up, so as not to appear broken, but I also want to keep it down so as not to draw attention to myself, therefore putting a target on my back. I would love to find, and stay, at that middle ground.

"Welcome to ND3," a woman says as she leans against the wall next to me. "What's your name?"

I am not happy with myself for becoming distracted and not realizing this woman was approaching until she was within shot of me. I've been taught well not to trust anyone. "The powers that be have given me the identity Inmate 8895."

"We like names around here," she says. "My name is Dena. How do we address you?"

"You may call me Artemis," I answer, with a calculated smile.

"I like you, *Artemis*. When you desire company, I am in the C-wing."

"I will keep that in mind."

"You do that." Dena laughs. "And it wouldn't hurt your case if you'd be a little more social."

"My case? I wasn't aware I had a case." I lift my foot to rest on the wall behind me, a move for both defense and comfort.

"Just like the guards, the other prisoners can make your stay here heaven or hell. It will ultimately be your choice. Play nice, or pay the consequences." She smiles big, showing a dark gap where she is missing a tooth on her right side.

"That, too, I will keep in mind," I say as I use my foot against the wall to propel myself away from the wall and Dena.

Despite the advice to be more social, I spend a lot of time looking at walls. Well, I am looking toward the wall but actually seeing everything that happens in my peripheral vision. That's how I came to know that Dena in the C-wing had a habit of putting herself in the middle of a lot of the drama behind the scenes at ND3. It seems Dena thinks of herself as quite the lover. By quietly watching, I also learn that there are some couplings in my wing—Alice and Barbara, Bea and Carli, for starters.

I am prone on my thin mattress when my bunkmate Bea comes in with her lover, Carli. I don't realize for several long moments that they do not know I am there. Once they start touching intimately it becomes awkward for me and I decide to stay very still and not draw attention to my presence. The sounds and scents of intimacy fill the cell and I don't know what to think about the flutter low in my belly.

The women in the bunk opposite grow quiet, then sit up and begin to adjust their clothing. On their way out, Carli pauses and looks right at me.

"Did you enjoy the show?" she asks.

"Yes, thank you," I say in my most confident voice.

"Maybe next time you'd like to join?" she asks.

"No, but thank you." And with that I take a chance and roll over to face the wall, leaving my back to the women, vulnerable to any attack they may have decided on. They leave without incident. I remain in my bunk the rest of the day, contemplating how the sounds I heard from Bea and Carli made me feel warm in my belly…and lower.

It is also while trying to blend into the background and watching everything in my peripheral vision that I learn to beware the male guards. If they think for even a second you are interested in them, they will get you into a closet and make you do things to them.

I am going to my bunk after my meal—a mushy concoction of different grains with a sliver of cheese on the side—when my attention is drawn to an incident occurring outside of the toilet room. I look up into the eyes of the most amazingly beautiful woman I've ever seen. I know I am supposed to avert my eyes away from the guard immediately, but I can't. I stare at the woman, helpless to look away, or breathe, or keep my world from spinning out of control.

When the guard stands in front of me, I finally look away.

"Is there a problem here, inmate?"

The woman might as well have grabbed me by the neck and choked me like the men in processing had, because I can't speak, can barely breathe, and feel my legs about to give out on me.

"I asked you a question, inmate."

I keep my eyes averted and attempt to swallow.

"No," I croak. I can feel my face growing hotter and hotter.

"No?"

I glance up briefly—into light gold-brown eyes—and grow even more confused.

"No, ma'am?"

The guard shakes her head. "What is your name, inmate?"

"I am Inmate 8895, ma'am." I wait for the tirade at not answering the question with my name.

"Go to your bunk, Inmate 8895."

I follow directions, but wonder if there isn't slight amusement in the guard's words.

It takes a while, but I begin to feel more normal once I am away from the beautiful guard. Can a person both love and hate how someone makes them feel?

Staring at the dirty wall makes my heartbeat slow down, but then I feel penned in. I hope to be put to work in the garden or the bird coop. It would be worth the risk of getting mauled by an emu to collect eggs for my keep instead of being stuck indoors. I glance up at the narrow strip of uncovered window. All the windows are mostly boarded up in ND3, and I am sure that withholding sunlight is but one way they slowly break us.

†

It is the next morning and I perch on the edge of my bed, waiting for the barred door to be opened by a guard. Bea goes to the toilet in the corner. I have not known anyone to use it except for Terry one night when she was ill.

Bea glares at me when I don't move. "You want to watch this, too?"

My face grows warm at her mention of my unfortunate audience while she and her lover were intimate. I glance around and see that everyone else is facing the wall. I lie back down and roll toward the dirty cinderblock. I stay like that until Terry and Maria have both taken their turns, then I sit back up and look again toward the door to the cell.

"You are waiting for the toilet room down the hall?" It is Maria who rolls over to look at me.

"Yes, I will wait."

"It'll be a long day for you, then." Bea laughs.

"I don't understand."

"Today is the Day of Atonement," Maria says.

"I still don't understand."

"It is the one day of the week that we are not allowed out of our cells. While the Anointed guards atone for their sins, we are locked away. They will send someone with one meal for us later." Maria shrugs. "So please, just use the toilet in the corner."

"Yes," Bea says without turning from the wall. "Just do so now so we can begin to let the stench of us all start to dissipate."

"Let's be done with it," Terry chimes in.

Maria rolls to face away from me.

I relieve myself and as I sit back on my bunk they all roll away from the wall. It feels awkward, but I jump right into conversation to take the attention away.

"Tell me about this Day of Atonement."

"It's their way of washing away the guilt of treating us like animals. Once a week they spend the day in ritual and prayer," Maria says.

"Like one day is enough!" Terry adds. "What they need is a month of atonement."

"We just wait here all day?" The thought of being caged with three others for a whole day is disconcerting.

"Yes, we do. So, we have all this time to get to know one another. Now is a good time for you to tell us your name," Bea says.

"Or where you came from," Terry adds.

"Or maybe we just enjoy some quiet, meditative time," I venture.

Maria finally breaks the tension. "We could explain to you some of the details of this hell hole. I don't know where you came from, who you are, or why you are here, but the bottom line is you are no better than anyone else in here and life can be pretty difficult if you aren't prepared."

"Thank you," I say, my voice low and a little choked. I know there is an insult buried in her words, but I also see an olive branch.

"Where should we start? *For God so loved the world…*" Terry scowled as she spoke.

Bea laughed, "My personal favorite is *You dare not hide your vile affections?*" She pretended like she was going to grab Terry between the legs and Terry let out a playful squeal.

The teasing doesn't last long and our harsh reality is soon addressed. On my first Day of Atonement at National Detention #3, I learn that it is illegal for an Anointed to reproduce with someone who is not Anointed. I learn that they rape us in ways that guarantee we won't get pregnant, and that it is helpful if the guards see you as too dirty to touch.

I learn that they call us all Pagans whether we are followers of the Earth Spirit or not. Jewish, Islamic, Buddhist, progressive Christians, and others are all considered Pagan here.

I learn that Isolation can break you, and that Retirement isn't really retiring to a different life, but being taken somewhere to be killed when you no longer serve a purpose. The trick is to stay healthy even if you don't think you'll be chosen for a work assignment, because as long as there is a possibility that you'll be useful, you will be allowed to live.

We grow quiet and I think about the beautiful guard with her pale skin.

"Where do the guards live?" I ask whoever cares to answer.

"Most of them live in the dorms on the farthest side of the facility," Terry says. "I've heard they have some pretty nice rooms. The higher-ranked ones have the choice to stay here or go home to Grover on their days off. Or so I hear."

"You sure do hear a lot," Bea teases.

"I used to fu—I used to be friendly with a woman who cleaned for them," Terry says.

"How does one get a work detail around here?" I ask.

"*One* behaves and gives a name when asked," Bea answers. "This isn't an employment camp, you know. Most of us are here because we aren't to be trusted."

"But some work," I say.

"Yes, some do. But I don't think anyone in this cell is work material," Bea says with a laugh.

†

I know I'm being watched on my ninth day as I spread the sheet I've finally been given over my mattress.

"What?" I ask, growing tired of the audience.

"I don't care if you watch, but you better not ever say you'd like to join in," Bea says.

"Ah." I know I need to choose my words carefully. "I don't care what you do with whom. I don't even care if you get off on an audience, but I'm not interested in either of you."

"Are you saying Carli isn't attractive?"

"I'm saying I'm just not interested in being with anyone in here."

"Because you're better than us?" Bea asks.

"Of course not. Because it's not my thing." I don't know if that is even true or not. I suspect that it isn't, given my reaction to both hearing them carrying on, and a single kiss from my dear friend turned potential girlfriend, Emily, but I sure don't want to get into all of that with Bea.

Later, on the way to eat, Bea and Carli step in front of me, halting me. Bea grabs Carli between the legs and Carli gyrates her hips.

"Oh," Bea says, "I'm not offending you, am I?"

"Not at all," I say, simply, as I step around them. Behind me I hear laughter. Would I be better off just coupling with someone and playing the part of lover to keep the others off my back? Although it sounds good in theory, I know I would never use someone like that.

I eat my boiled egg and toast in silence, and as I'm on my way out of the dining area, a spontaneous head count is called. I line up along the corridor with the others.

I know better, but I watch as the beautiful guard's gaze scans the prisoners. The woman wears her long blonde hair twisted into a knot at the back of her head. I run my hand over the stubble on my own head and wonder what the guard's hair smells like.

We are lined up to be inspected by the guards, and as always we are to look straight ahead, not address them, and not make eye contact. Even without looking, I always know when it is the beautiful guard standing off to the right of me. I think to read the name badge hanging around the guard's neck, but know if she looks up and somehow meets my eyes, I will fall to my knees or hyperventilate.

I feel her presence. I listen closely, and hear the other guards call her "Heart." How appropriate, I think, since the mere sight of her causes my heart to beat recklessly in my chest.

I must stop thinking of Heart like that. I distract myself by reflecting on how I am growing weary of not having anything productive to do. Why have they not given me a work assignment yet? Isn't that the whole idea of imprisoning the "others" in this dichotomy of a world we live in? I decide when the count is complete that I will look around more of my wing of the prison. It wouldn't hurt to get an overall layout of the place in my head.

As I walk down the corridor that I believe leads to the laundry, a woman I've never seen before steps in front of me.

"We knowin' your name isn't Artemis," the woman says.

I shrug, and continue down the corridor. My mind is trying to place the cadence of her language but I can't come up with the region she is from.

"Don't you dare walk away from me when I'm talkin' to you."

I hesitate just briefly, but then decide not to engage the woman. I veer left and take a detour back to my bunk where I sit on the edge of my mattress. Again, I think about making up a name. If I give my own, I will likely die in the dump they call ND3 before the Resistance can break us all free. But still, I worry about hurting someone else by making up the wrong name.

The bell signifying dinner rings. I am on my way to the dining hall when a group of women, seemingly led by the one who most recently accosted me in the corridor, approaches.

"So, ladies, this new punk is needin' to be taught a lesson about respect."

I square my shoulders as I look over the four other women, hoping to see a face with even a little compassion. I do not find any such expression.

"Yeah, Leona, teach her a lesson," a near-toothless woman says.

"So, Artemis, I'm givin' you one last chance. What's your real name?" Leona asks.

"It is fine that you continue to call me Artemis," I answer.

Someone laughs.

"Don't be laughin'. It's not funny," Leona says.

I study this woman, Leona, memorizing the slightly asymmetrical features of her face, then look quickly at each of the others, knowing it best to be familiar with the faces of those who are not your friends.

"Excuse me," I say, as I try to maneuver the space between them and the wall.

"I'm not excusin' you," Leona says. She shoves me against the wall.

Before I can even raise my hands in a defensive position, the others are upon me. There are so many fists and feet coming at me all at once that I can only twist and try to break free, at least enough to get my arms over my face.

I am on the ground then, and through the forest of legs I can see Dena in the background, not joining in, but not helping me either. Carli puts her hand over her mouth, and then runs down the corridor, presumably for Bea. She only half-heartedly tries to help me when she arrives.

"Okay, that's enough," she mutters, without taking any action on my behalf.

The air is forced out of me with a powerful kick to my stomach. I try to breathe, try to protect my head with my arms while curling my legs into a fetal position to protect myself from further kicks to my gut. There is so much going on around me, causing me to grow dizzy. I can feel one eye swelling shut, and I try to look out of the other but blood stings that one when I open it.

I smell cigarette smoke right before I feel a searing pain against my arm. Although substantially more intense, it reminds me of my first bee sting at the huge hive in Karst—. This is much more like a betrayal than the sting I'd received when I didn't pay attention and got too close to the swarm.

My pants are now around my knees and I feel something being pressed between my legs. An excruciating pain sends my body convulsing and my mind mercifully goes blank. I am suddenly back in Karst, my favorite place in the world, with Suzanna, one of my favorite people. Every time I relax into my fantasy the pain comes harder and I am returned mentally to the disgusting floor in the filthy prison with these horrible women.

My arms are pulled away from my head. I lash out at my attacker as I open my good eye just in time to see my fist make contact with a guard's arm. I have struck Heart.

A male guard is on me in no time. He presses my head into the floor with one hand, and catches my fist in the other. He kneels on my back. His bulk on me is overwhelming, causing breathing to grow difficult. I panic.

He wrenches my arm backward while pressing harder into my back with his knee. I hear it, seemingly before feeling it, as my shoulder is ripped from its socket.

"Shit," the man grunts.

"Get off of her," Heart says.

Pain overtakes me and all goes black.

CHAPTER TWO

I regain consciousness as I'm roughly deposited on the thin Med Center mattress. I know my shoulder is either dislocated or broken. I hope it isn't the latter. I stare up at the dirty, water-stained ceiling and clench my teeth against the pain.

"Inmate, what is your name?" a guard asks.

"I am Inmate 8895, sir," I say, my voice weak.

"Inmate," this time the man speaking has a stethoscope around his neck. "This is going to hurt like hell."

I open my eyes and although the one is still swollen shut, the other has been cleared of my blood, and I can see quite well through it.

"Can you give her something first?" Heart asks.

I turn my head to better see the beautiful guard. Her light golden-brown eyes seem almost copper now.

"No," the doctor says, effectively dismissing Heart. "You hold her head still and pin down the other arm. Jones, you hold down her legs."

I feel Heart's hands on my forehead and good arm. The sensation of her touch sends an undeniable warmth throughout my body.

The doctor climbs onto the cot with me, straddling my torso.

"What the hell?" I ask, as I try to buck out of their grasp.

"Shh, hold still." The soft voice sends warm puffs of air against my ear. "They have to put your shoulder back into its socket," Heart says.

"Okay," the doctor says.

I take a deep breath and concentrate on how close Heart is. If I turn my head just right I could press my lips against hers.

The pressure against my chest grows nearly unbearable, but I don't want to cry in front of Heart.

"Listen to me," Heart says, her one hand moving slightly against my forehead.

I concentrate on the soft voice.

"It will be over," Heart says.

Oh no, no, no. Oh, the pain. I squeeze my eyes closed against the sensation of my bones being torn apart.

"In no time," she continues. "See, it's done."

"We could just put her down like a lame horse," says the man who is holding down my legs.

"Are you kidding me? Did you see how she handled that pain? We'll make one hell of a worker out of this one." This person I can't make out.

"Breathe," Heart whispers.

I do. And it hurts. Everything burns.

Heart caresses my forehead for a brief second before releasing her hold on my head and good shoulder.

"Who did this to you, inmate?" Jones asks.

I stare straight ahead, barely registering the guard with the white hair and gray eyes, again focused on the stained ceiling, not acknowledging the question.

"Okay, have it your way."

"Let me talk to her," Heart says.

I turn my head away from her.

"You don't get it, do you?" Jones asks. "These are pagans. They are like animals; they will just keep attacking each other and never say a word about it. Unless it's a guard, then they go crying to other inmates about how horrible we are. Let it go. I did my duty and asked. We're done here."

"Good, you're done. Now everyone out," the doctor orders.

"Patch her up good," the person out of my sight says. "I have just the work crew for her when she gets out of Isolation."

ISO? Oh, right, I struck Heart. I thought I was defending myself from my attackers and instead I struck Heart, a guard. I turn and watch as she leaves the room. When she glances back briefly and makes eye contact, my stomach does a little flip. Then she is gone.

The doctor immobilizes my shoulder, then begins taking off my pants.

"Hey," I complain.

"I need to clean you up and examine you for internal bleeding." He spreads my legs. "Quit fighting me, or I'll have to put you in restraints. Is that what you want?"

"No," I whisper, beginning to panic. "Please, no restraints."

He touches me between my legs and I close my eyes and try to imagine being at Karst with Gotham and Breanne, visiting with Suzanna and my friends, Heidi and Dawson.

The doctor slides something cold and hard inside me and everything goes black.

When I next awaken, I am alone in the Med Center. My whole body aches.

The door opens and the doctor walks back in. He gives me a few sips of water. "How do you feel?"

"Like I've been hunted down by a pack of coywolves… or beaten by a bunch of prisoners and guards."

He ignores my words, and writes a few notes on what I assume to be my record. He hands me a bedpan.

"Here, in case you need to relieve yourself. Try not to get any on your sheets, because they are the only ones you'll get in here. Oh, and urinating will be quite painful for a while."

He leaves the room again and I squeeze my eyes shut.

Sometime later, I wake and hear the doctor giving someone a rundown of my injuries.

"Massive internal tearing from the inanimate object she was assaulted with, the shoulder injury, eight stitches above her left eye, chest and abdominal contusions. Oh, and some cigarette burns on her arms and—well, other places."

It hits me then how lucky I am to be alive.

"And," the doctor continues. "She may have a concussion, possible facial fractures."

"What will be done about that?"

I gasp at the sound of Heart's voice.

"Nothing. She's just a pagan worker. If she were Anointed we'd send her to the hospital in Grover, but she's not, so we're not."

"How long will she be in here?" Heart asks.

I am so preoccupied with hearing Heart's voice that I miss hearing the doctor's response.

After, for days, I lie there and hope Heart will show up. I do not hear her voice again in the Med Center.

When a man who is not the doctor removes my sutures, he is rough. I don't let the discomfort show on my face. I will not give him that satisfaction.

Day after day, I grow more and more disappointed, and eventually aggravated, as I walk laps around my room, feeling horribly stir crazy and angry with myself for thinking that the guard Heart might come back to check on me. *Stupid*, I chastise myself.

I then choose to appreciate the peace and quiet, the private toilet, and the chance to regularly sponge bathe myself.

†

"Up, up, up," the guard named Jones sings as he comes into the Med Center. "Today is transfer day."

"Transfer?"

"Yep, off you go now to Isolation. The good doc has given his seal of approval for your release from medical care. So, off you go to pay for your bad behavior."

I sit up and swing my legs over the side of the bed. He throws some clothes at me. "Put these on."

I look at the clothes, then at him.

"Oh, you want some privacy?"

I start to nod my head, forgetting for a fraction of a second that I get nothing from these people, I am nothing to these people.

"Inmate, you don't get privacy." He kicks the side of my cot. "Now get your ass up and get changed."

As soon as I am dressed, he leads me to the Isolation wing. The air is heavy with mold and unclean bodies. I fight the urge to gag. There are large insects scurrying about and the light is dim. I imagine it is quite dark at night and wonder how I will fare in the horrid, unfamiliar conditions.

Someone whimpers as we pass. Another woman in another cell is screaming for someone to get the damned rat out of her space. I hesitate when I hear that, so the guard pushes me forward.

"And here is your new home," he steps aside and gestures for me to go in. "Get in there, I don't have all day."

He stops in the doorway of the small cell. "Inmate, what is your name?"

"I am Inmate 8895, sir." I stand at attention. They may have taken my freedom, but I will not freely give them my name.

He steps out into the corridor and slams the metal door behind him.

I am thankful that I am able to continue to bite my tongue and not ask why they bother to assign us inmate numbers if they are so preoccupied with our names. I look around the cell. It is barely eight feet by eight feet, but aha, another toilet to myself!

A concrete slab built into the wall serves as my bed. I wonder if they will eventually bring me a mattress or pad for it.

I glance around, thinking about how small the cell is. It is not lost on me that the confined quarters could make one go mad. I sit on the hard slab and wipe away tears. I can't afford to be saddled with thoughts of not making it out of this place sane, or not making it home at all. Instead I force myself to think of the antics of my brother, Gotham, and sister, Breanne, twins who are five years older than me. Gotham and Breanne showed me parts of the world that were secrets kept from Father and his Resistance diehards. I miss the twins more than I miss my oldest brother, Lewis. Lewis and father have a harder edge to them than Gotham and Breanne. I have always adored the lighthearted, genuinely kind twins.

Growing up, I was closest to Breanne, Gotham, and my cousin, Camryn. I started scouting on foot with all three of them, albeit not at the same time, but ended up doing my work alone. Long before the twins stopped joining me, Camryn had to stay behind at the homestead because she couldn't keep up. At least that gave my cousin more time with her beloved books. I got so good at walking long distances and climbing obstacles that it didn't take long before the twins joined me on horseback, then quit going with me at all. Their time was better spent going to Karst or some faraway area to barter for produce.

Although the twins quit scouting with me many years earlier, I know I would not be in the predicament I am had they been near. Or would we all be imprisoned together now? No, there was no way the twins, at least not Gotham, would have allowed themselves to be taken alive.

"Viajar con seguridad." *Travel safely.* "Gute fahrt." Camryn has books in many languages back at the homestead. Each time before I would leave on a scouting mission, she would tell me some variation of "travel safely" in a different language. I miss my cousin and all her languages.

The window slides open, leaving a small square of bars and letting in a minute amount of light.

"Inmate, identify yourself," the shrill female voice commands.

"I am," I pause, thinking to use the term "prisoner" since the guards insisted on calling us inmates. I think better of it. "I am Inmate 8895, ma'am."

"What is your *name*, inmate?" she asks, louder.

"I am Inmate 8895, ma'am."

"You do not care to eat, inmate?"

"Yes, I would like to eat." I take a tentative step closer.

"What is your name, inmate?"

"I am Inmate 8895."

The window slides shut with a loud clank, leaving me in darkness. I know I could just make up a name, but I refuse to give in. Besides, what if the name I fabricate belongs to someone whose life is ruined by it being recorded that she was here, at this time, in these circumstances?

I return to the hard cement slab serving as my bunk.

At least, I tell myself, I have the better sense than to lie and tell the guards my name is Artemis, as I did with Dena. Ah, Dena. I think about her watching from the sidelines while I was attacked by the other prisoners.

"If you aren't a part of the solution, you are part of the problem," I whisper.

I will never forget the faces of the attackers I did see, and will learn not to trust, thanks to the faces I didn't see. I do not want the black rot of revenge settling further in my heart, so I distract myself by thinking about the quiet times around the fire in Karst, listening to the stories of the elders and sipping on honey-sweetened water.

†

It is hard to calculate the passage of time as I sit in Isolation and try to control my breathing. The second or third day has my hunger echoing in my belly.

The cell is so small, the air is stale, and I can't shake the feeling that I'm being watched. I glance again at the small window and see nothing there but the metal that slides back and forth from the outside. My gaze flits around the room, and in the low light I make out the silhouette of something small, possibly hunched. It moves along the far wall and I am sure it is a rodent, probably a rat.

"Hi, Dawson," I whisper, surprised by the smile that forms on my face.

Back at Karst, our dreamer, Suzanna, not only dreams of others' past lives, but can look deep into you to see your soul's animal mate. Once, while gathered around the candles and incense with a group of friends, Suzanna offered to name our animal mates for us. I never felt the need to hear of my past lives from Suzanna, but the prospect of knowing my animal did interest me.

Everyone laughed when she told Dawson his animal was a rat. He'd shrugged it off in true Dawson style.

"And look at how my rat relatives still thrive, long after other species have left us for good." Then he'd pulled his partner Heidi closer and asked, "What animal is my love here?"

"Heidi, give me your hand." Suzanna took my best friend's hand in hers and began to anoint her with lemon oil. "Ah, but of course. You are an elephant."

"An elephant?" Heidi and Dawson asked simultaneously.

"They are extinct," Heidi said, sadly, "but I remember from my lessons that they were generous and intelligent animals. Oh wait, weren't they afraid of rodents? I have no fear of Dawson."

"You should fear me, I am the almighty King of Rodents!" Dawson puffed up his chest and narrowed his eyes.

Heidi slapped him playfully.

I remember now, sitting on the floor of this tiny cell, how ecstatic I was for my friends. Their love for one another warmed my soul then, and warms it now.

"Inmate!" The window slides open and I jump up.

"Identify yourself!"

"I am Inmate 8895, sir."

The window slams shut. I sit back down and close my eyes, let my mind drift back to Suzanna and her animal mates. She'd turned to me next. "Love, shall I tell you what your animal is?"

I smiled and nodded to Suzanna. Gotham had joked often that I was part camel so that is the answer I expected. I wondered if there were any camels left in the far reaches of the world, but knew no one could know for sure.

"Yes, Suzanna, please tell me my animal."

Suzanna took both of my hands in hers and closed her eyes briefly, then opened them and stared at me for a long time. She rubbed lemon oil along the palms of my hands and started to hum an unfamiliar tune.

"You are a coyote."

"Coyote?"

"Yes, love, long before the coywolves, there were coyotes, wolves, and dogs. The wolves were fearless. The dogs, loyal. The coyotes—they were the most cunning."

"Cunning," I had repeated. "What happened to the coyotes?"

"The coyotes bred with the wolfdogs that came from the breeding of wolves and dogs. Without the combining of bravery, loyalty, and intelligence, they would have all died out. The combined DNA was resistant to the great rabies." Suzanna brought my hand to her cheek and pressed it there for a moment.

"Resistant and stronger? Like we are now that we have combined races?" Dawson asked.

Suzanna just nodded, maintaining eye contact with me.

"Unlike the elephants and the Anointed," Heidi whispered.

I close my eyes and whisper, "I am Coyote."

†

The window slides open.

"Inmate!"

"Yes, ma'am." I jump up. I know that voice and it makes my heart pound harder in my chest.

"Inmate, identify yourself," Heart says.

"I am Inmate 8895, ma'am."

"What is your name, inmate?" her voice is harsher now.

My mouth grows dry. My desire to please her is just slightly less than my will to survive.

"I am Inmate 8895." I struggle to keep my voice steady.

"Please," the guard named Heart says, her voice low and pleading. "You must be starving."

"I am very hungry," I admit.

"Identify yourself and let us be done with this nonsense."

"I am Inmate 8895," I say, my voice now a hoarse whisper.

The window slams shut and I choke back a sob. Several moments pass and the window slides slowly open, barely registering a sound.

I cannot hear nor see anyone. I hope it is Heart coming back, as I have not had the chance to apologize yet for hitting her. I hope to finally work up the courage to address her to say I am sorry.

"Who is there?" I whisper. I stand off to the side, out of range for fear of being struck or sprayed.

When no answer comes, I move my head to see out the edge of the window. My breath catches in my chest. It is her, as I knew it would be. The light outside my cell reflects off Heart's pale skin. She is so beautiful.

"I didn't strike you on purpose," I say.

"It is policy that you come to ISO for striking a guard," she responds.

"Yes, I know that. But you must know that I did not strike you on purpose."

"It does not matter. It is policy."

"It matters to me that you know that I would never do anything on purpose to hurt you. Please, tell me you understand that." I am powerless to keep the pleading out of my voice.

When no answer comes, I add, "I'm sorry. You weren't hurt badly, were you?"

"No, I was not hurt." There is movement and I back away slightly. "Come to the window, Inmate 8895."

Ignoring the pounding in my chest, I step forward. From my position this close to her I now notice that she is a couple of inches taller than I am. A piece of bread appears between the bars. I stare beyond the bread, into the shadowed eyes of the woman. I can barely breathe.

"Take the bread."

I stare into those eyes. I don't know what color they are now, just that they are beautiful.

"Don't make me throw it to you like an animal." The tone in her voice jolts me from my staring.

I take the bread, watching the guard closely.

The window closes and I let out a breath, a painful, sobbing breath. I devour the bread, barely chewing it. Then I slide down to the floor and cry until I fall asleep, propped against the filthy wall.

I jump when the window crashes to the side, waking me.

"Inmate, on your feet," the deep male voice orders.

I go to the corner, as far from the window as I can get, and stand at attention.

"Inmate, identify yourself."

"Inmate 8895, sir."

"What is your name, inmate?"

"I am Inmate 8895, sir."

The window slams shut. I know I will go another day without a full ration of food. I sit on my bunk, the cement pressing my bones, and wonder if Heart will come to me again.

Just after the evening count, after my refusal to give my name, and the subsequent withholding of my rations, the window quietly slides open. I again stand off to the side of it.

"Who is there?"

"Come closer," the whispered voice says.

I smile when I recognize it as Heart. I move closer to the barred window.

"You came back."

"I do not know if I will be able to again after tonight. Here, have a sip."

She hands a small metal cup through the bars. I cradle it in both hands, with her fingers still holding the handle that sticks straight out from its side, and bring it to my lips. The honey-sweetened water tastes so good that I am almost overwhelmed. I blink back the stinging from the tears and look into her eyes. The pain I see reflected back at me makes my throat tighten.

"Thank you," I whisper.

"Take this." She nods her head slightly.

Bread and cheese appear between the bars. I grab it, and immediately feel poorly for acting so.

"Thank you."

"When you are removed from here, you must immediately go to supply and ask for menstrual items."

I am of that population that doesn't menstruate, cannot bear children. "But I don't –"

"No matter. If you are a breeder, the male guards are less likely to come to you in the night when you are transferred back to general population. You must act like a breeder whether you are one or not. Go to your bed now."

I bring the bread and cheese to my cement slab and barely register finishing it when I am awakened by loud voices outside my cell.

CHAPTER THREE

My head is sheared again before I am sent with the others to the shower. I hold on to the ring above me, hold my breath, and shut my eyes just before the stream of water assaults me. The burst from the hose stops sooner than I expect and I open my eyes to find a guard standing just inches away from me.

"Well, don't you clean up nicely?" he says, looking me up and down before turning off the water and setting the hose down on the floor behind him.

The tension around me is palpable.

I think about letting go of the ring to shield myself from what I assume is his intent to touch me, but know if I do, and the hose starts again, I can be seriously hurt. I've seen that enough times to know better.

"Not too bad, for a pagan," he says. "I must say you look better than most of the pagan mutants."

The women around me shift uneasily and I feel my face growing hot with rage.

He roughly grabs my right breast, and then laughs. "I know you like that," he says.

Just as I was taught about dealing with wild animals, I do not make eye contact. I peer over his shoulder and see Heart. My teeth clench. My only hope is that if I am to be raped that Heart doesn't see. I can't bear the thought of her witnessing my shame yet again. Anger burns my face as the man gropes my other breast.

"Come on," Heart calls out. "That's enough, we have a job to do."

"I'm busy," he calls back to her.

I startle when one burst of water hits the guard on the back of his knees. Heart has picked up the hose.

"Knock it off," he says.

"*You* knock it off," Heart responds, sending a burst of water to the floor just an inch from his feet. "We have a job to do."

"We aren't done," he says to me. He spits on me, hitting me just to the left of my navel, then steps back.

He walks away, and when the water comes back on, it's in a steady spray, not as harsh as usual when it hits me. I can feel the spit washing off, and for that I am grateful.

On the way out of the shower, Heart hands out clean prisoner uniforms. My flesh burns when Heart's hand grazes mine as I take the clothing. I do not look up, not willing to risk making eye contact, not able to look at her without feeling the shame of having that man's hands on me.

†

Upon being assimilated back into general population, one of the first things I do is go to Supply and ask for some tampons and napkins. I have no idea how to use these items, but make a show of getting them anyway.

A male guard eyes my new stash of items as I bring them to my bunk. In a sudden flash of brilliance, I put my hand to my lower abdomen as I've seen other women do during that time. I throw the items down on my mattress and make a mental note to give them away. I will try to remember to go to supply every month to continue the charade.

Over the midday meal I hear rumors about a work detail being put together to go to the nuclear cleanup site, and I have a good idea why I've been transferred out of ISO. It's not going to do me any good to start worrying about this now, so I push it out of my mind.

A guard I've never seen before approaches me with a mop. I look away as he speaks.

"Inmate, bring this to the maintenance supervisor. She's waiting near the laundry. Go straight there and come straight back."

I reach out for the mop and he jerks it away before my hand makes contact with it.

"What did you say?" he asks.

"Yes, sir." I reach again and this time he shoves it at me, jamming my thumb. I resist the urge to look up—and the urge to kick him in the groin.

On the way back from the laundry corridor I see Heart in the hallway. She appears to be waiting. My chest starts to pound and my stomach does this little lurch thing that I don't understand.

"How are you?" Heart asks.

I know she is referring to the shower incident. I cannot look at her. I want to thank her for the food in ISO, the interference in the shower, giving me the idea to act like a breeder, and the general show of kindness, but I can't speak at that moment.

My emotions confuse me.

"Settled back in?" she asks, her voice gentle.

"At least there is a mattress," I say, finally finding my voice. "Unlike the concrete slab in ISO."

"If you had not gone to ISO you would have been targeted even more when you returned from Medical. The other inmates would have been suspicious."

"I know." I swallow hard. "Thank you."

"Do not thank me. I followed policy."

I glance up at her, making eye contact for the first time in this conversation. "Yes, but you could have—"

"Inmate, stop." Heart's voice is hard, but does not match the softness in her eyes.

I do as I'm told and stop discussing that. But I don't want to end the conversation yet, so I blurt, "I would do just about anything to spend some time outside."

"You can only do so if you are chosen for a specific, outdoor work detail."

"How do I make that happen?"

"It is too soon. They will want to vet you further. It does not bode well for you that you will not identify yourself when asked."

"Is there a less formal way to spend a little time outside?" I ask. I am overwhelmed with the desire to be outside under the glorious sun with this woman. She is so pale, so fair, I wonder if she goes out into the sunshine at all.

"You are asking me how you can sneak out?"

"Yes, I am asking you that."

She cocks her head and says, "I cannot in good conscience tell you how to break the rules."

"I would take to the grave the information as to how I found out how to accomplish my goal." My voice might convey a touch of humor, but I sincerely mean this.

"I do not worry about you informing on me. I do worry about you going to your grave for a few minutes of hot, dusty time on the outside."

"And if I thought it was worth the risk?"

"I cannot understand why you would think that. That would be foolish."

"You find me foolish?" I ask. The humor is leaving me.

She studies the floor in front of her feet.

"Do you believe me foolish for being a dirty pagan, or foolish for getting caught and brought here?" If I dared to touch her I would lift her chin and make her look me in the eyes.

"I do not think you are foolish. I think you have been through a lot and might have foolish ideas about what things are worth dying for."

"What do you think is worth dying for?" I ask.

She looks up and stares at me for several long moments but does not respond. When the alarm for a head count rings, she looks away finally and says. "I am sorry I angered you."

"I am not angry," I whisper to her retreating back.

As the next day is a Day of Atonement, there is plenty of opportunity to reflect on the time I have had with Heart. I want to see where she sleeps, know how her time is spent when not working in this awful place. When I close my eyes I can see her image against the inside of my eyelids and it leaves me feeling breathless and ragged along the edges.

†

The days are all so similar that they blend together until they are but a blur. The only day that stands out is the Day of Atonement, but even they all look like each other before long.

After a month and a half of incarceration, as I can best tell the passage of time, I have taken to wandering the halls, always looking over my shoulder, but looking for something I have not yet figured out. I eye the women going to work on the laundry detail. That is a much coveted job, one that doesn't come easily.

It is during one of my wanderings that I feel I am being watched. I press my body against the filthy wall of the alcove at the electrical room and wait. When no one immediately comes past, I feel perhaps I'm being paranoid. I'm about to peek back down the corridor when I hear a familiar voice.

"Are you looking for something or someone in particular?" Heart asks.

"No, I am not." I step out into the corridor and my heart pounds wildly when I see she is smiling. "I do expect to know it when I see it, however."

I am pleased when that is received with a widening of her smile.

"How are you today?" she asks.

"I am fine. And you?" I prop my boot behind me against the wall, trying to look relaxed.

Heart assumes the same position against the wall opposite me. "Fine as well," she says. "What is your name?"

"I am Inmate 88—"

"Stop it, please. For my ears only. When I silently wish you well at the end of the day, what should I call you in my prayers?"

I stare at her. I desperately want to trust this woman, but I know I should not. My mouth opens as if to speak, but no sound comes out. Breathing becomes difficult.

"Why do you look at me like that?" she asks in a low voice.

"I don't look at you in any way." I rip my gaze away from her. I don't want to think about, let alone discuss, the way looking at her makes me feel. I search for another topic of conversation.

The lights flicker and the bell sounds. Heart frowns.

"It is time, Inmate 8895, for the evening count."

"Am I meant for the nuclear cleanup crew?" I ask. I don't want our brief time in conversation to end.

"Yes, I believe you are. I am sorry." Before she looks away I see the sadness in her eyes, the same look I saw when she gave me the drink in ISO.

"I will miss you when I go."

"Are you scared?" she asks.

"No. Yes. Not really. It's not like I'm leaving behind anything here." As soon as the words are out, I feel mean. I want to take away any possible sting, but don't know how to. I feel my teeth pressing against my lower lip as I reach for her hand. "I mean—well—"

She squeezes my hand gently. "I understand."

"I will miss running into you—totally unplanned, mind you—in the corridors."

Her laugh is beautiful music. She quiets for a moment. "I will miss our time as well. I will miss you. I—I —"

"Me, too," I whisper. I allow my thumb to run along the edge of her finger as I continue to hold her hand.

She looks away. "Go, it is time to stand for the count."

We go our separate ways. I keep my eyes averted as the guards do the count and give us our daily smudge of tooth gel, and then head dutifully toward my cell. Heart's eyes haunt me. I am both happy and sad that she looks distraught at my upcoming work detail. A lump forms in my throat. People do not come back from nuclear cleanup. When I leave, I will die out there. We all will.

I enter the cell quietly and notice Maria shoving something under her mattress. My curiosity is piqued, but I am not one to meddle. She is startled when she sees me, but I do not show any signs of having seen her hide anything. Terry and Bea enter behind me.

I stretch out on my bunk. As it often does during quiet times, my mind goes to a more peaceful place. I think about Karst and Emily. Remembering Emily's kiss makes me tingle, just like the kiss itself had. I roll over and close my eyes, meaning to relive the sweet kiss I shared with Emily the last time I was at Karst. Against the black of my closed eyelids, I will the image of Emily to come to me more clearly, but it is not her I see. It is not Emily's full lips or her slender neck that I see. Heart's image appears in my mind and my entire body tingles. I quickly open my eyes and try to still my quickening breath.

Soon it is lights-out. Terry, in the bunk over me, has begun pleasuring herself each night before sleeping. I am forced to lie awake, unable to dismiss the sounds as anything but that, until she is done. Some nights it makes me want to touch myself like that, but the urge doesn't linger unless I am thinking about Heart. But I cannot entertain those thoughts about the beautiful guard without feeling shame, so I push them out of my mind.

†

Within a week, I break my own rule and look under Maria's mattress. She has hidden a blade there, made from one side of the shears they use to cut our hair short. It has been sharpened enough on one side to be a fine weapon. I leave it be because, even if I am a snoop, I am not a thief.

Maria comes in moments later and I am glad to not have been caught looking under her mattress.

"How are you?" she asks

"I am fine. You?" I smile at her.

"Fine as well." She doesn't hold eye contact.

"Something on your mind?" I ask.

"I just hope you are no longer a target. Leona's type doesn't let go of their hostility easily."

"And what is Leona's type?"

"Feral," she says, as if I'm daft.

That explains the accent I couldn't place. "Feral, in here?"

"Oh, yes, and she isn't the only one. They rounded up a group five or six years ago. Split them all up to keep them from packing together and becoming dangerous."

The Ferals do not embrace the ideals of the Resistance or the Anointed. They are a dangerous bunch, only out for personal gain, and they are violent and ruthless in pursuit of that gain.

Maria takes her leave of me and I decide I need to move around a bit as well.

As I meander the corridors, I walk past the toilet room and hear someone vomiting. I briefly weigh whether I should see if she needs help, then decide if it were me I'd rather be left alone. I continue on, albeit slowly.

Behind me I hear a familiar voice. "Do you need to go to Medical?"

I stop in mid-step. Heart doesn't sound like an Anointed guard, she sounds like a regular, caring person.

"No," the inmate says, surprise evident in her voice.

I turn toward them in time to see the inmate standing in the doorway of the toilet room and Heart offering her something. The inmate, I see now it is Alice, hesitates at first, then takes what is being offered and puts it in her mouth.

Heart walks away and I approach Alice.

"You are all right?"

"Yes." She is moving something around in her mouth.

"What did the guard give you?" I ask.

She works something green to the front of her mouth and presents it through her teeth, then shoves it back beside her cheek.

"Lemon basil."

"Basil?"

"Yes, when chewed it's lemony. It's to rid my mouth of the taste of being sick." She smiles. "That guard isn't so bad. Just don't tell anyone."

Her secret is safe with me.

Alice takes leave from me to go lie down and I resume my wandering.

When I see the Feral woman, Leona, victimizing someone else, I become enraged. Has she not learned anything about how this bullying escalates? Does she not care? Of course she doesn't—she is Feral.

I grab Leona by the arm and throw her against the wall. She holds her hands up in surrender. Studying the Feral's face, I cringe at how a smile seems to play at the corners of her mouth. I could just let it go, now that she has backed off the other woman, but I am reminded of the constant pain deep inside me from when this woman shoved the broom handle into me, leaving splinters and ripping my insides. I snap.

My fists find Leona's face over and over and when she falls to the ground I kick her in the stomach several times. Bile burns my throat as I stand over her. I look around at the audience that has gathered and I glare, daring anyone to come at me.

I know instinctively that no one will rat me out because I did not name my attackers after my beating. I am well aware that is the way of things in this horrible place.

Back in my bunk I am ashamed and hope that Heart never learns of the violence I gave in to this day.

My knuckles are bruised. Some of the other women pretend not to see the proof of my rage. I don't care. Maybe it's best they think I'm a monster, maybe it will keep them away from me. The only person I hide my hands from is Heart. I do care what she thinks of me.

†

It is confirmed. Heart has whispered to me that I am to be sent to the nuclear site in just three days' time. At least I know, at least I won't be surprised like the others when the guards come for them with no warning. I glance around and wonder who around me will be going outside to be worked to death with me.

I am both terrified and relieved by my assignment. I'd rather die out there working than in this dark hole. The only regret I have is that I will miss seeing Heart across the room or hearing her voice when she breaks protocol and speaks with me.

I am making peace with my new reality when the woman who had steadied me the day of my first shower, the one whose kindness kept me from falling on the slippery floor, approaches me. She whispers to me that freedom is on its way. I don't know why she is sharing this information with me, we have had no contact since the event at the showers. I do not even know her name.

When I hang out around the electrical room next, Heart does not come. I am disappointed and don't stay long. On my way back past the laundry room there is a cart of laundered inmate clothing outside the door. I am suddenly aware of why I have been wandering—I know what I need to do.

The shirt I steal fits under my own without showing too badly. I return twice more to steal a pair of pants and another shirt. The second shirt, I hope, will be bartered for the next item I need to act on the plan I now have.

It takes most of the afternoon, but I am finally alone in the room with Maria. I like her as much as I can let myself like anyone in this place. I hope I have read her well and can appeal to both her honesty and vanity.

She has just gotten prone on her mattress when I ask, "How much longer before showers?"

"Excuse me?" Maria startles and I realize she had not known I was sitting on my bunk.

"I hate how ripe I get between showers." I pull at my shirt.

"Yes, I know what you mean." She smiles.

"If I knew how to get you a fresh shirt would you be interested in a barter?" I ask.

"You have a clean shirt?" She sits up on her mattress.

"Barter?" I smile.

"I do like you," she says, looking down at her feet. "But I—I am not into women."

I stare at her for a long time before I can fully grasp what she has said.

"Oh—no, I—I didn't mean *that*." I feel my face heating up. "I just thought maybe you had something you'd like to trade for it." I let my eyes flick to the end of her mattress where I've seen her hide the blade.

Her eyes grow wide at the realization that I know her secret.

"You think I prefer to be clean more than safe?" she asks as her body turns rigid.

"I mean no disrespect." I fear I've lost her.

Her shoulders relax a little.

"I would be willing to use your—your tool—to protect you should the need ever arise."

"If you know my secret why haven't you just taken it?" She cocks her head.

"I am a lot of things, Maria, but I am not a thief." Now I cock my head.

"I'm sorry," she says. Tears spring to her eyes. I have never seen her cry and it affects me in ways I'm unfamiliar with.

We sit quietly for a moment. Finally she whispers, "You have the shirt? Really?"

"Yes." I lean toward her slightly. "All you need to do is keep your old one in your bedding until shower day. Then stuff it under your newer shirt when we get called to the shower and just toss it into the laundry with what you are wearing. No one has to know but us."

"It's a deal."

As I am pulling the clean shirt from under the blanket at the foot of my bedding, I see her looking. There is nothing there for her to see as I have hidden the other shirt and pants elsewhere. She pulls the blade from under her mattress and I put it in my boot, careful not to let the sharp edge touch my skin.

I wait until later in the day to sneak away to put the blade with the inmate clothing I have stashed in the ceiling above one of the toilets. I am now ready—if only the army comes for us before I am made to leave for the nuclear cleanup site.

At lights out, I am crawling onto my bunk when I hear Heart's voice outside our cell. I can't make out what she is saying, have no idea to whom she speaks, but just knowing she is so close, yet untouchable, makes my chest ache.

I stare at the bottom of the upper bunk. My body, hell my very soul, reacts to this guard in a way I can't understand and can't stop craving. To find someone you want desperately but know you cannot have—someone you can never get close to—and then to lose them, is devastating.

My mind forms the thought, unbidden: I would trade my soul for a chance to satiate the yearning that just being close to Heart creates.

To just press my lips against hers once…

I close my eyes and her image plays against the inside of my eyelids. I press my fists against my eyes in an attempt to chase away the longing and regret.

My right fist leaves my eye and goes to my mouth where I try to contain the choked sob that is so close to escaping.

"Hey." It's Maria's voice. "You all right?"

I squeeze my eyes tighter and do not respond.

CHAPTER FOUR

It is nearing the day I will be sent to work on the nuclear cleanup site. I've been holding out so much hope that the Resistance Army would come before now. I have my plan in place with the prisoner clothing and weapon, and will not give up hope until I am marched with the others out to be worked to death.

Yes, I might die on the work crew, but the army might come on time as well. I am prepared for either. If I am sent to the nuclear site and cannot escape on the way, I will die at peace with the way I have lived my life. If the army comes on time I will implement the plan that is taking shape in my mind. My breath grows ragged as I try to imagine Heart going along with what I have planned…

I am pacing the corridor, wanting to see Heart one last time before I am to go. If the army does not make it in time, I want to steal a kiss from the beautiful guard before I must leave. If the army does come, I hope I will be able to find Heart in order to implement my plan.

I hear a series of small explosions off in the distance. It sounds like they are at the outer doors to the prison. Lights flicker. Inmates and guards run in all directions. My heart slams against my chest wall.

Maria stops as she runs past.

"They have come for us! Our army has come for us!" She bounces slightly on her toes. "Come on, come with me to freedom."

"Are you sure?" I smile at her excitement. I cannot risk exposing my plan if this is not what it appears.

"What else could it be?" Maria looks confused.

A guard runs past us, blood on the front of his shirt, panic etched on his face.

From the direction he came, we hear a commotion.

"Resist! Welcome the Resistance!"

Prisoners break out in cheers from the direction of the day room. A man in a dark green uniform stands at the end of the hall. Maria and I both smile.

"Go, go to freedom," I encourage Maria.

"But you must come, too."

"I will be along shortly. Go." I give her a nudge.

Maria kisses my cheek, then runs down the corridor toward the Resistance soldier.

I run in the opposite direction, through panic and chaos, until I see who I am looking for. Heart uses a towel to stem the flow of blood coming from a wound in another guard's abdomen. The arrow that protrudes from his flesh looks ominous.

I am heartbroken when I see the sheer terror on Heart's face. Grabbing her arm, I pull her to her feet and am surprised when she allows me to lead her to the east corridor.

I pull her into the toilet room and she shakes free from my hold.

"Stop, please, what are you doing?"

"The Resistance soldiers are here to liberate us," I say.

"Then you must go."

"Please, come with me."

"How can I possibly leave?"

I had not considered in my planning the prospect that she wouldn't let me save her.

"How can you stay? You won't be safe here. I've always heard that anytime there's a shift in power, it gets more and more brutal for the oppressed."

"They won't let me leave," Heart says.

I climb onto the toilet, pop out the loose board in the ceiling, and reach up to pull the stolen prisoner's clothing from its hiding place overhead. I hold up the clothes.

"They will let us leave. We leave together, as freed prisoners." I climb down and softly stroke the side of her face. "I'm afraid for you if you don't come with me."

"Why are you doing this?" she asks.

I look away, not wanting Heart to see on my face the feelings I have no way of controlling.

"Why?" she asks.

"Because I don't want you to be harmed after I leave."

"I don't understand you," Heart says.

I place my fingertips under her chin and steer her face toward mine.

"Because I want you with me," I whisper. I bring my lips to Heart's and let them linger there, barely touching, before pressing them together for just a moment.

"Why?" she repeats. The color rises on her face.

I don't know why she keeps asking this. Have I made a huge mistake in thinking she would want, accept, my help? I fight to breathe.

"Don't you feel this?" I stare into her eyes for a long moment. *Please tell me you feel this.*

She leans in to kiss me. When she pulls away, she turns her head away from me.

"Please."

"Please leave you alone? Please never do that again? Please let you die here with your people?" I speak through gritted teeth.

"No, I mean please turn and give me a little privacy," Heart says, one side of her mouth twitching as she seems to fight a smile.

I quickly turn to face the other direction. I am vulnerable with my back to this guard as I watch Heart's shadow dancing on the dirty, crumbling wall in front of me. Would I know with enough time if the shadow were to show Heart coming at me in attack? How would the shadow on the wall appear if she uses the time I am turned away to run away from me? I push away all doubt because how can I possibly ask Heart to trust me now if I won't trust her?

"Okay," she says behind me. "You may turn back now."

I turn slowly and let out a relieved breath when I see Heart in the prisoner's uniform I have stolen for her. "Very good. Now your hair."

"My hair?"

"The only way you look like a fleeing prisoner is if you wear the same haircut as I do." My hand goes to my head in a movement that mirrors Heart's hand to her own. "I'm sorry, but we must sheer you." I grab the blade from its hiding place in the corner under the sink.

Her skin is so pale, so delicate, as if the sun's rays have never been allowed to strike her.

"Please. We must do this now." The fear I see on her face as she stares at the blade is a kick to my gut. Voices rise in the background. Time is running out for my plan.

"We must hurry," I plead.

I steer Heart to sit on the edge of the toilet and begin hacking off big sections of her beautiful, fragrant hair. Each time a clump falls, I watch it land on the filthy floor. Before taking the last strip away, I hold it to my face and inhale. Heart smells lemony.

I run the blade over the last of her hair, then trace a finger along the line of her jaw, my fingertip lingering under her chin, along the slight ridge of a small scar. She continues to stare straight ahead, just as she had the entire time I ran the blade through her hair.

"Are you okay?" I ask.

Heart turns to face me. Her eyes hold something I don't recognize and I find myself losing control, as I always do when I look into her eyes. I believe this is a woman who has no idea how strong she is, no idea the power she holds over me.

Loud voices ring out down the corridor. I force my gaze away. We don't have time for me to try to make sense of my reaction to this woman. I hide the blade in my boot.

I jump up, spit onto both of my hands and rake them down the dirty walls. Then I step up to Heart. "Sorry," I whisper before smearing spit and dirt onto her face, taking care to blend around the newly shorn hairline to hide the newness of the haircut. I drag my dirty hands down Heart's neck. When I feel her blood pulsing under the skin on her neck, I press my fingers into the flesh slightly, unable to stop myself.

The voices are closer. I turn away from Heart and shove her guard uniform behind the toilet. At the last minute, I snatch up Heart's name badge.

I pause at the entryway and look down the corridor. "Come. Quickly."

We walk out into the corridor where a guard is sprawled on the floor, holding his arms against his head for protection. Two prisoners pause over him. I see the deep scar on his forehead, just above where his arm futilely tries to cover his head and face.

"Leave him be," I order, thinking about the mercy Cooper showed me during my first shower.

They stop and study me. I glare at them and they leave him there, and then we move down the corridor, toward the outside world.

Farther down the corridor, deep into the building, we come upon a group of prisoners kicking a prone guard. I recognize him as being one of the most brutal of the guards, the one who groped me in the shower. I nod approval at one of the prisoners, and then step around and past them.

"Come, come." When Heart stops near an obviously dead guard, I grab her by the arm to hurry her along.

I clutch Heart's name badge in my hand. *R. Hart.* I had the spelling wrong, but to me it will always be Heart. I tuck the badge down the front of my shirt. I don't dare leave it behind, so I take it and plan to find a fire in which to destroy it.

"What does the R stand for?" I ask as we near the open courtyard outside of ND3.

She stares at me.

"Please. What will this world call you?"

"Rachel."

"That's beautiful." I smile, then lean in and whisper in her ear. "I am Kai."

PART TWO—LIBERATION

CHAPTER FIVE

Together, Rachel Hart—Heart—and I step out into the bright sun. Heart stops in her tracks as she puts her hand up to her eyes.

Soldiers on horseback are everywhere. I remain vigilant—hyper aware—as I watch the armed Resistance soldiers round up the Anointed, stripping them of their weapons, and shoving them toward the detention center doors.

Heart watches me at times, looks down at other times. I can tell the sun is bothering her.

A soldier rides up on horseback, and I call up to him.

"Please help us. We've been in solitary confinement for so very long. The sun… it hurts us."

"Here, sisters." The soldier reaches behind himself and grabs two headscarves. He tosses the headwear down and I catch them both.

"She's so weak," I say as I reach to put the scarf on Heart. She looks at me and her eyes are gold, amber, and copper, all at the same time. I swallow hard. "I will help her first."

"Of course. Cover up, then go to the registration tent. If you are able to walk, there is a warehouse serving as registration a few miles to the east. It won't have the long wait of this first one."

"Thank you." I finish wrapping the scarf around my head and neck. "We will walk to the next registration area."

"Resistance forever," he calls out as he pounds his chest and turns his horse away.

"Resist!" I hit my chest with my hand.

Heart's fingers go to a smudge on her cheek. I recognize that there is something so intimate about the act of spitting on my hands to rub dirt onto her face, but when I'd done it nothing seemed more natural. Heart, on the other hand, had looked totally off balance by the action.

A tall, large-chested man walks toward us. I step protectively in front of Heart. The man embraces me, and says, "Welcome to freedom."

"Thank you," I say, breaking the contact and bowing slightly.

The man embraces Heart then. When he pulls away he stares into her eyes for a very long time. I am about to distract his attention away from her when he finally smiles.

"Welcome to freedom."

"Thank you." Heart mimics my slight bow.

I take her by the hand and lead her toward the east. Our feet break the dry cakes of arid earth with every step. When Heart peers behind us and sees her people being herded into the detention center, my chest heaves.

Ahead, a pair of crows bicker over a piece of litter. I am so happy to see the obnoxious, intelligent birds again. I look up and try to find other birds. None are in our immediate vicinity but I know the vultures, falcons, and sparrows are around somewhere. The few species of birds that remain have adapted well to the harsh environment of New America.

My attention goes back to Heart. She is wide-eyed, maybe even in shock. I wonder if she feels the same hatred toward my people as I do toward hers. Does she feel overwhelmed by hatred for the Resistance soldiers, for the ugliness of some of her own people, and for the evil system that has pitted otherwise decent people against each other?

The line at the first registration center is long, as expected. I recognize my fellow prisoners and know we must move past quickly if Heart is to be safe.

"Are you okay?" I ask. "Can you keep moving?"

"I am fine. I can keep going." She gives me a small smile.

The sun is getting lower in the sky. We probably won't make it to registration before dark. At least it is not as bright and Heart doesn't have to shield her eyes so much now.

"This is better?" I ask. "Not so bright?"

"This is better." She smiles and my insides flip and flop.

"You'll get accustomed to the sun."

"The sky, it is changing colors."

"Yes, it will be a beautiful sunset."

"What will happen?" Her eyes grow wider.

"You've never seen a sunset?" I stop and gently touch her arm to stop her forward movement as well.

"I've not seen much of the sun since I was a child." She cocks her head. "I've never had reason to be outside late enough to see it become night."

I turn her to face west, into the orange and red streaks of the nearly setting sun. I glance around and see that others have also stopped to enjoy the view. I realize my hand is still on Heart's arm. I slide my fingers down to her hand and am relieved when she allows me to intertwine my fingers with hers. It is like this that we watch Heart's first sunset.

The sun has just kissed the horizon when Heart gasps. I see a tear is streaking down her cheek. I want to show her everything she has missed. I want to hold her hand, just like this, and show her all the beauty that remains in our world.

The sun disappears and she turns to me.

"So beautiful."

"Yes, beautiful." I mean that she is beautiful, but I am fine with her thinking I mean the sunset we just shared.

She hugs me and my heart pounds in my chest. I want to stand in her embrace all night long, but touching her like this makes my legs feel weak and I know we cannot afford that. We need to make it to the registration area soon. I reluctantly pull away.

"Thank you for this," she says.

"I can't take credit for the sunset." I smile.

"Thank you for caring enough to talk me into leaving with you."

"Thanks for trusting me enough to come." I look around at others still watching the changing sky and know that many haven't seen it in years, decades even, unless they were out on a work detail. "We must go."

We walk the remaining distance with very little light. In near silence, the only sound is the crunching of the ground beneath our boots. I am full of mixed feelings when we finally approach the registration area.

Temporary lights are set up in a perimeter around the large warehouse that has a roof over only half of it. Tarps cover gaping holes in the walls. There are a few people in line in front of us at the makeshift shelter as we approach. I recognize the woman whose UV tattoo is being applied from ND3. I glance at Heart, but she is looking down.

What relief I had felt starts to nag at me. I feel the flesh on the back of my neck crawl. Without knowing why, I start to lead her to the right, away from the registration tent. I hope she doesn't recognize how my breathing has quickened.

"You there!" a soldier calls to us.

I hesitate. I cannot afford to make an error in judgment now.

"You must go to registration," the soldier says.

I nod and redirect us back toward the tent.

"Don't be afraid," I whisper.

"What if someone recognizes me?" she asks.

"It's fine. Come," I urge her forward.

We step up to the table. The man reaches for the box of old data cards to his left as I indicate with a nod the scanner he has just set down on the table.

"Oh? Come closer please," the man at the tent says to me. I step closer and pull my shirt away from my shoulder. He waves the black light scanner over the UV ink barcode otherwise invisible on my skin and gives a little jump when a low ding surprises him. I am pretty sure no one expects anyone coming out of a detention center to be in the system that was just recently put into place.

"Kai Brodie?" he asks as he stares at the display on the wand.

"Yes."

"As in Winthrop Brodie?"

"Yes, I am related to Winthrop Brodie." I feel my face growing warm.

"Yes, of course. Of course!" He nods his head enthusiastically. He calls over his shoulder, "Clark, this is Brodie's kid!"

The second man comes over and extends his hand. I shake it briefly.

"Wow, this is a surprise," he says. "So, we need to update your data. All Resisters are to be scanned and updated." He shakes his head. "I can't believe we have a Brodie here. This is exciting."

"If it pleases you, I have had a rough time lately and just wish to get home." I am uncomfortable with the attention.

"Of course." Clark looks from me to Heart and my stomach knots. He types information into his handheld, then turns to Heart.

"We will be heading to the Brodie homestead now. Is there any news of it?" I know a distraction won't help much, but I try anyway.

"Yes, indeed." He taps the scanner against the palm of his hand as he speaks. "Your father was with the liberating army, as was your brother, Lewis. I know nothing of your other siblings, I'm sorry to say."

"Thank you for the news of Father and Lewis."

Clark looks again at Heart. "Who is this?" He reaches the scanner toward her shoulder.

Heart takes a step backward.

He reaches to the box of data cards and looks at Heart. "Last name?"

"She's with me." I stand straighter. "She won't be in the system."

"Oh, I see." The man extends a clipboard. "You have to register all property. No exceptions."

I take the offered clipboard and write a few fictional things on it, including classifying her as an undocumented pagan instead of an Anointed.

"You want her registered in your name, or your family's?" Clark asks as he takes the clipboard back.

"Mine only." My head pounds and I cannot believe what I have just had to do.

"Very well." Clark enters the information from the clipboard into the handheld. He picks up the tattoo hand piece and steps closer to Heart.

She reels around to glare at me.

"It's okay. It doesn't hurt badly," I try to reassure her.

Heart starts to back away, but the man grabs her by the headscarf and pulls her shirt off of her shoulder. She struggles against his hold on her.

"No, stop," she pleads.

My heart breaks for her.

"Hold still," he demands.

"It's okay. Just be still." I step forward and take Heart's hand.

Her lip trembles as her eyes plead with me. "But—"

I can only imagine how confused she is by being called my property, but I will explain it to her once we are alone and she will be at ease in no time. Or so I hope.

Her eyes squeeze shut as the UV ink is tattooed onto her shoulder.

"Done," Clark says. He rubs some antiseptic over the site. He extends his hand to me. "Remember to keep close tabs on her. You're responsible for any damage caused by your property."

"Good night to you," I say as I shake his hand.

"Take some provisions from the other table. There will only be a few places offering food and beverage until you get to town or your homestead."

"Thank you."

"There has been much concern for you. Many feared for you when you disappeared."

"I am well, as you see," I say.

"Yes, well, and with property," he says, nodding his head.

I hadn't been sure, but had figured there would be some procedure in place for undocumented people, especially now with the power shift so new. Surely Heart will understand why I have to register her as my property. If she had known this was how it was going to be, would she have left ND3 with me? If I had known, would I have told her?

Heart doesn't look me in the eyes the entire time I gather our provisions and strap them to both of our backs. I include one lantern, fastening it to the side of the pack I carry. I pick out two long-sleeved shirts and hand one to Heart. She doesn't take it right away.

"I know it's hot but you will need to keep your arms covered so they do not burn in the sun."

She slips hers on and I do the same. At the last second I grab two rain slickers from the table and add them both to my pack, just in case the weather turns earlier than usual.

I turn and gesture for Heart to walk. We are a few yards away from the men and the tent when I stop. Most of the people leaving the registration area are walking northwest, toward Grover. I believe we are better to go due north, just to the east of the North-South Highway, even though the rising altitude makes it a harsher route. It will rejoin the highway past where most others will have turned off for Grover. Then we can follow as it arches northwest, south of Mt. Sanders, to the Brodie homestead from a point farther to its east. I believe this route will keep us from walking with those who may recognize Heart. Even with her headscarf, it's risky.

Decision made, I place my hand on her elbow to indicate we should start walking again.

"Do not touch me." She jerks away from me.

Laughter rings out behind us.

"Oh, she'll take some breaking," Clark says to the other man.

After walking in silence for about an hour, I pause at a fire pit on the side of the road and burn Rachel Hart's name badge.

"Now, I no longer exist," she says through gritted teeth.

"Now your identity cannot hurt you. Your new name is Rachel Prince. That is the name on your registration."

She glares at me.

"It's just a formality," I whisper. "Just to keep you safe."

She has turned away from me. I start walking without another glance at her or the burning name badge. I hold out hope that she will one day soon understand and forgive me. But if not, I can try to find peace in the fact that I have done my best to protect her.

†

The trek is not easy and is made harder by the darkness. I decide we have enough distance between us and ND3 to stop for a rest. I begin to scout for a suitable camp area as we walk. I can see another fire ahead; this one has armed guards around it.

I think to stop before we make it to them, but once I am sure that they have seen us, I decide to keep going. I would rather approach them and leave, than have them come to our camp and make it more difficult to take our leave from them.

"We will go just past the fire up ahead."

Heart does not respond.

"There are guards or soldiers there. Let me do the talking." When she doesn't respond again, I add. "You heard me?"

"Yes," she barks in a harsh whisper. "Loud and clear."

"Good evening," a soldier says.

"Good evening," I answer. "We are passing through."

"Well, well, who have we here?" Another soldier steps closer.

"We must scan you or see your papers." A third soldier elbows him.

I step closer and pull my shirt off my shoulder.

"Nice," the second soldier says. "Maybe you two want to hang around here with us for a while? We can party?"

My shoulder is scanned and the soldier with the device turns to the foul one. "Shut up," he warns.

"What? Why wouldn't we want to pass the time with these hot women? What do you say, sweetheart?" he asks me.

The other soldier holds up the scanner for his comrade to see.

"Oh, I'm so sorry, ma'am." He pounds his chest and says, "Resist."

I mirror his gesture.

"You're headed home?" the first soldier asks.

"Yes, we are."

"Give our regards to the General." He looks over at Heart and nods.

"I most certainly will." I look at the man who'd been less than respectful just a moment earlier.

"Do you need water?" the first soldier asks.

"No, we are fine." I do not require a lot of water while hiking, one of the reasons my missions prior to being incarcerated were so successful. I am an efficient scout, but have been trying to encourage Heart to remain hydrated. "Do you have any cheese or egg you can spare?"

"Yes, yes of course." He offers up a satchel with both and I tie them to the side of my pack.

"Thank you," I say.

"My pleasure. Beware the coywolves; they have been quite active lately."

"Thank you, I will take seriously your warning."

We take our leave and I am glad they chose not to scan Heart after scanning me. She'd looked terrified the entire time we were engaged by the soldiers.

I keep us moving until we are out of sight of the men. Then I stop and point to a log on the side of the road. "Let's rest."

Heart adjusts the weight of the pack on her back, and almost falls before she gets to the log. I grab her around the waist to steady her.

She recoils at my touch.

"Hey, I didn't mean anything by that," I say, not making eye contact. "I was just trying to steady you."

"I am sorry if it is unclear to me what is going on…Master."

"Don't be cross. It was the only way. Would you rather be in a cell? I could have left you at ND3—at the mercy of the new regime."

"ND3 is all I know," she says.

"You know me," I respond in a strained voice.

"No, I do not know this version of you."

"I'm still the same person." I sit on the other end of the log and adjust my boot.

"No, you are not. Power changes everything. And everyone."

I do not respond as I am tiring of the matter. Eventually, Heart too sits on the log and adjusts her boots.

"Do you want to walk through the night?" I ask.

The widening of her eyes gives me the answer.

"We will sleep until first light then." I glance around. "Near that stand of trees."

She follows me, a few paces behind, and stops when I do. She follows my lead on using the pack as a pillow. We bed down without further talk.

†

The next day we walk in near silence until we find another good spot for camping. And then, at first light the following morning, we eat a meal of cheese and egg. Then we begin walking again, this time joining up with the North-South Highway and following it. I slow down slightly to help Heart with the increasing incline of the dusty road we follow. We've gone another several hours when Heart stops short.

"Who is it? What is happening?"

"The welcome wagon has arrived." I smile.

"Do you know him?" Heart steps behind me.

"He's my nephew, Sebastian."

The boy jumps off the huge stallion and throws himself at me. I hug him tightly, then as if coming to his senses, he abruptly pulls away.

"I'm almost a man."

"Yes, Seb, you are." I laugh. He seems to have grown several inches in the mere months since I last saw him, and is almost my height now. "I am so happy to see you."

"I'm happy to see you, too." He smiles. He cranes his neck to see Heart.

"Ride back, tell your grandfather I will be there shortly."

He nods and jumps back onto the horse. As he rides away, I point off into the distance.

"See the rock formation on the horizon?" I don't wait for her to answer. "Just beyond that is our destination. We will be there shortly, then we can rest."

A small gray cloud has settled over us and within minutes a light sprinkling begins. I think about the rain gear in my pack and decide if it comes down any harder I will pull the slickers out for us to slip on.

We continue our hike in the light drizzle and in a few hours we approach the three large boulders. Heart's gaze moves up the side of the mountain just beyond the towering rocks. Her eyebrows knit together when she next looks at me.

"We are not going over the mountain," I say, hiding a smile.

She glances to the left, then the right.

"And we aren't going around the mountain."

Now she looks directly at me.

I can no longer hide the smile.

"We are going through the mountain." I reach to take her by the hand, then pull away. "Follow me," I say, embarrassed that I've been caught up in the moment and almost touched her.

I am taking a huge risk allowing Heart to see access to my family's homestead. I know this, but I also know I am responsible for keeping her safe, with or without her blessing.

"We will go through a tunnel and come out the other side." What I don't bother to tell her yet is that the mountainside is rigged with leg traps, snares, camouflaged pits, and all other barbaric means to keep people from getting too far up and over the mountain where our homestead would become visible.

"Welcome to Witches' Peak."

Her eyes grow wide. "Witches?"

"It's just a name. Some people feel it necessary to label places and people when they don't understand them. And some people," I gesture with my arms to include myself and the general vicinity around us, "allow others to believe what they want."

I watch her for a reaction, but if she has one she hides it well. The Anointed always assumed witches and black magic ran rampant in this area because they couldn't explain the disappearance of their soldiers every time they tried to summit the mountain.

I light the lantern I've been carrying and I see by her expression she now understands why I would not use it while we traveled in darkness.

"Stay behind me, don't veer off to either side." I lead her around the boulders that hide the opening of the tunnel.

The lantern gives an eerie glow to the narrow, dirt walls of the passageway. The dank smell plays with my memories. This was once the smell of a mission accomplished, of coming home after what were usually long, tiring treks. Now it is also the smell of apprehension, of the unknown. It feels closer to the smell of the confinement at ND3 than the liberty it should evoke.

Heart stays close behind me as we walk, and I am sure the dark dampness of the tunnel frightens her. I have a thought about her trying to leave the homestead without me, stumbling around the base of the mountain and being injured. I must make her understand.

"The mountain is booby-trapped. Anyone who tries to climb it to get in or out of our complex will be trapped, and either killed or severely injured."

I glance back at her and witness her shudder.

We walk the remaining distance in silence. When we exit the tunnel the precipitation has already stopped. Heart holds her hand near her eyes for several moments. I walk slowly, giving her time for her eyes to adjust to daylight again.

"Halt!" Jonas, one of my father's most trusted soldiers, steps in front of us and looks at me with his eyes narrowed.

"Does that thing work or do you just think it's pretty?" I look at his ancient rifle.

"The General will see you now." He scowls, creasing his forehead right above his bushy eyebrows.

I almost laugh, but decide not to push Jonas's buttons today. I lead Heart away from the soldier as I note that I don't like the way he's looking at her. I know I must get accustomed to the way men will look at Heart, for she is beautiful, and her light, smooth skin is quite foreign to most of us.

Sebastian is waiting outside my father's living structure.

"The General is waiting inside for you!"

"Thank you, young man." I pat his back as I pass him.

I hold the door for Heart, but then step past her immediately before we are upon the general.

"Father," I say, as I give him a stiff bow.

Winthrop Brodie places a hand on each of my shoulders and holds me at arm's length. His square-jawed face shows no sign of any emotion.

"Ah, the prodigal daughter returns. And what have you brought me?" he examines Heart as he speaks.

Heart takes a step back.

"Corner. Now," I order her.

Heart's expression shows shock, and I assume she is taken aback by the tone and the coldness, the way I don't look her in the eyes. She moves to the corner as she's told.

I stand straighter. "She's mine. Registered solely to me."

"I do believe I'm proud of you." He laughs.

"That fills my heart," I say, letting the emphasis rest on the word "heart." My feelings are hurt that he hasn't really inquired about my well-being. I continue. "Tell me about Lewis, Gotham, and Breanne."

"Ah, the motley crew I call my offspring. Shine?" he asks me. He takes his glass from the table.

"No, thank you."

"Lewis will return shortly. I've heard nothing of Gotham or Breanne." He gulps from his glass. He studies my face. "You've had a time of it, yes?"

"Nothing I couldn't handle." I square my shoulders and angle my head upward to look him in the eyes.

"You did not finish your last mission. What became of the note you were to deliver?"

"I ate it when I became compromised."

"You've been missing for months. Where were you held?" he asks.

"ND3."

"Did they know they had Winthrop Brodie's child?"

"No, sir."

He raises an eyebrow.

"I was Inmate 8895. Sir." I feel a little sick to my stomach, knowing things could have been much worse for me, had they known that I am this man's daughter.

"Very well. Clean up for dinner. Secure your property in your bunk."

"Come," I say. I head toward the door.

Heart jumps at my tone, and follows me out the door, into the darkening evening. When I pause at the door to my small cinderblock hut, she looks around frantically.

"It's okay, go inside."

Heart clenches her teeth. Her hands ball into fists at her sides as she follows my orders. I enter and lock the door behind us.

The small room with separate toilet and bathing area is exactly as I left it. The walls are painted and clean. The floor, made of polished wood, is dusty from time passed, but not dirty in the way that the prison floors were. I am not surprised that it is unchanged. Winthrop Brodie has always been secure in the hold he has on his daughter, never thinking I would leave and not come back unless rendered incapacitated. I feel a little sad as I wonder if my father worried at all for my safety when I didn't return, or if it was just the note I carried that concerned him.

I forage through the portable wardrobe pushed off to the side until I find items I believe will fit Heart.

"You can bathe first." I hold out the clothes. I nod toward the door to the bath. When Heart doesn't make a move toward it, I say, "Go. The facilities are pretty self-explanatory. Call to me if you do need any assistance."

Did I imagine Heart cringing slightly? Of course she did—of course the mere thought of me going into the bath while she was in there was cringe-inducing.

"Please, be quick and come out when you are finished."

I throw pillows and blankets into the far corner, then pull out some clean clothes for myself.

Heart comes out of the bath, and I look up before quickly looking away again. With her cheeks pink from cleaning, she looks like an angel. I do not trust my own expression.

"I will have to bind you while I'm in the bath. No one should come in, but just in case, we will need you to at least look secure."

Heart cowers into the corner when I approach her with the rope. After binding her wrists loosely in front of her, I pick up my clean clothing and disappear into the bath.

I step under the stream of warm water and sigh as it hits my back. I've never been happier to be in my own shower. The shower stall is small, but private, and oh so clean.

Without warning, I find myself wishing Heart was with me in the shower. I imagine her golden eyes, then they change to the coppery-amber they are in the daylight and my hand slips between my legs as I scrub myself. My hand lingers and I close my eyes, enjoying the soft touch. But then the image of her bound in the next room assaults me. I shake it off, then begin to lather my shorn head and body with the citrus-scented soap. I wonder how long until my hair grows out.

The warmth of the water loosens the tightness in my shoulders. I stand in the shower longer than is conscionable, and tears start to flow. I am sad for all the families torn apart because the people of New America—the Resisters, Anointed, and all those in between—are scared and selfish. I cry for the lost intimacy with Heart. I cry in relief to be away from ND3, in fear for Heart's safety, and in sadness that there is so much danger and hatred in this world.

I adjust the temperature and let the cold water pelt my face for a moment. There you go, shake it off, I tell myself.

When I come out of the bath, Heart glares at me. I feel the heat of her anger burn in my chest.

"I really am sorry, but I must leave you like this for now. I'll leave this knife with you, under the pillow, if the need arises to flee. And by *need*, I mean my death or disenfranchisement."

"How dare you?" she asks.

I flinch. "I'm sorry. It's just while I attend to some business with my father. I'll figure something out so we can stop with the bindings after this. I promise."

"You promise?" she hisses. "Did you not promise to protect me when you convinced me to leave the center with you?"

"That is exactly what I am doing." I turn to leave. "Get some rest. I will return soon."

I dread meeting with the others, but know the sooner I get it over with, the sooner I can get back to Heart. I hope no one goes into my bunk while I am otherwise occupied. I lock the door with the key, knowing it is not the only key to the door, then slip it into my pocket.

I enter the meeting space and smile at Sebastian. He gives me a slight smile in return, but then his attention goes to the other young people in the room. My cousins Josh and Wesley are also twins, something that runs in the family. The young men eye me cautiously, but I don't blame them for being uneasy, considering the speculation that probably surrounded my absence.

I glance around at the other occupants. I am related to most people at the homestead, all but a few soldiers, like that vile man, Jonas, my father has allowed to make their home here.

"Have you heard that we have finally gotten technology back on track? Well, not on track but definitely closer than ever," Uncle George says.

"What do you mean?"

"General Grayson has gotten a computer network up and running. He's even made it possible for the scanners to send information to the mainframe at Sergeant Grayson's settlement."

I think about my tattoo scan, the updated data, and about registering Heart. At least I changed Heart's last name on the registration. I hope my internal panic isn't showing on my face.

"Well, we knew it was only a matter of time. We are Resisters, after all, smarter and more logical than the Anointed and their archaic beliefs." The general watches me as he speaks, his dark eyes boring into me. "You were scanned again, yes?"

"Yes."

Father nods and his facial expression seems to relax slightly. "Do you and your—property—find your bunk sufficient?"

"Yes, Father, it is fine. I would like to leave in a few days to search for the twins."

"Have you considered that perhaps Gotham and Breanne do not wish to be hunted down by their family?" Father asks.

"If I find them well but unwilling to return with me, then I will take leave without them."

"As you wish," Father says. "Now, shall we eat and drink to our hearts' content?"

There is a flutter in my belly and I wonder if it was to be an ongoing reaction to the word "heart."

"I would love some food, but no drink. I prefer not to start my time home with alcohol sickness."

He nods his head, but his narrowing eyes contradict his gesture of approval.

Camryn, the daughter of my father's deceased brother, brings forward the food. "You look so tired, Cousin. Are you sure you are well?" she says in a low voice, keeping the others from making out her words. When she leans forward her straight, black hair moves like a veil to give us a semblance of privacy.

"Yes, I am well. I'm feeling stronger every day I am away from the hell they call ND3."

Camryn winces. "They hurt you."

I don't respond, knowing it isn't a question, and that Camryn does not really want to know the sordid details. I gently squeeze my cousin's hand.

"But I am free now."

"Bienvenido a casa," she says. *Welcome home.*

"Gracias," I say with a smile.

I eat the stew, then prepare a bowl for Heart.

"You didn't say how you came about your new property," Father says.

"That's a long story—better left for another time," I answer, hoping he won't press.

"Ah, so you are planning for 'another time' here at our homestead, even after you go to find the twins?"

"Yes, of course," I answer, knowing in these erratic times it may or may not be true. "Good night, all."

I take my leave, and watch that no one follows me back to my bunk. I steady the large bowl of steaming food as I unlock and open the door before maneuvering my way in. I stop short when I see Heart, unbound, standing, and wielding the knife.

"Good, you are awake," I say, trying to keep my voice from betraying my alarm.

"I could kill you right now." She thrusts the knife in my direction.

"Why would you say such a thing?" Her words stab at my heart. I glance briefly at her face, then bring my attention to the knife. I place the bowl of stew on the table to the left of the door.

She stares at me. She is obviously thrown off balance by my lack of a reaction, and I use that in my favor, rushing at her and easily reclaiming the knife. She scurries into the corner, down on the bedding.

"I brought you some vegetable stew. Eat while it's still warm." I hope I am adequately hiding how my heart pounds in my chest.

Heart turns away and faces the wall.

"Do I have to throw it to you like an animal?" I ask, using her own words against her.

She spins around.

"Take it. Eat," I say. "You will need your strength." I hold the bowl up to her. I hand it to her, then go to the lone chair by the table near the door and sit. I use the blade of the knife I'd so easily taken from her to pick pebbles from the soles of my boots.

When she finishes eating the stew, she sets the bowl to the side.

"Sleep now. It has been a long day."

Heart turns onto her side, facing the wall. I gather the bowl and spoon and only hesitate for a second before leaving the room without binding her.

I close the door behind me and begin to walk to the kitchen area. I hear voices coming from my father's lounge. I cannot help myself, and stop to listen.

"The Revolution has been a success. Now we must start focusing on the Re*so*lution."

"And you still think you can get General Grayson's full cooperation?" asks a voice I don't recognize.

"Yes, I will convince him that resolution is more important than controlling the enemy," Father says.

"Very good," the other man says. "Once we dispose of all the Anointed, we won't have to worry ever again about the tide turning. There will be no tide to turn."

The stew in my gut starts to unsettle. What was this Resolution? It can't be what it sounds like, right?

"And your daughter's property?"

Blood roars in my ears and I have to concentrate to hear my father's response.

"It is obvious to me that she's Anointed. I will let Kai have some fun with her before I break the news to her."

"She will not like losing her property."

"She will get over it. Kai is a good little soldier. If I ask her to sacrifice her property, she will." Father chuckles.

"I'm sure you are right, sir."

I do not continue on to the kitchen, but rush back to my bunk. When I come in I am relieved to see no one has entered in my absence, and that Heart still rests on the blankets. I lock the door and put the dirty bowl back on the table. She looks at it, but does not ask why I have returned with it.

I settle on the bedding beside her, closing my eyes and concentrating on steadying my breathing. When Heart rolls away from the wall and lies on her back, I pretend to be asleep. A few moments later, she turns to lie facing me. I keep my eyes closed and my breathing steady. I know she watches me, and I let her do so undisturbed.

Three hours later, in the darkest part of the night, I rise to prepare to leave. Heart sleeps on her back, oblivious to my preparations. The woman must be exhausted, I think, knowing how hard it must be for her to be so totally out of her element.

I pack a few items into a duffle bag and a backpack from the bottom of the wardrobe. I want us to have a change of clothing, but don't want to weigh down the packs any more than necessary. Carrying water and food is more important. I grab two pairs of eye shades, knowing Heart will find relief with the tinted glasses once the sun comes up.

I study the boots in my wardrobe and wish I had enough for us both to wear a fresh pair.

I had wanted us to have at least a partial night of rest before leaving, but now regret not leaving earlier. My father's words—*resolution, sacrifice*—assault me and I think I might vomit. I fight the desire to be sick. I don't have time to show weakness such as that.

"Heart," I whisper, while kneeling beside her. "Rachel."

She awakens, startled, and I place my hand over her mouth to quiet her.

"Shh. We don't want to wake the others."

Heart twists her head to the side and I let my hand fall from her mouth, hoping she won't make me regret doing so.

"What's going on?" she asks in a whisper.

"We must leave now. Go to the toilet to relieve yourself, quickly though, and then we will leave."

When Heart returns from the toilet, I have the new boots ready for her.

"Try these," I say, hoping they won't be too small.

"Will they work for you?" I watch anxiously as she tries adjusting the laces to make room for her feet.

"They are a little tight," she whispers.

"But too much so?" I really want Heart to be able to use the gift of new boots I am offering. "Maybe they will stretch out in time?"

She shrugs. "Possibly."

I examine the two old pairs of boots. Heart's are in slightly better shape than mine. We really don't have room in the packs to bring old boots, but I am concerned about keeping us both comfortable enough to make the long trek.

"Are you willing to try wearing them, and if they start hurting your feet we can switch?"

"As you wish."

I wait for her to add "master" and even though she doesn't, the slight intonation makes me feel the sting of the unspoken word.

I slip my foot into Heart's worn boot, pull it out, put on another pair of socks, and then put both boots on. This will have to make do.

When we step out of the bunk, into the dark night, I can feel her confusion. I place a finger to my lips to signal to her the importance of being quiet as we leave the compound.

CHAPTER SIX

"Why did we leave in the middle of the night?" We have been hiking for about four hours before Heart speaks.

I jump at her words. It is the first time in a long time that she's addressed me other than in response to something I've said.

"I decided it was safer." I don't want to worry Heart by telling her what I'd overheard about the plan to exterminate all the Anointed. I am still hopeful that I misunderstood what I heard, but must take all the steps necessary to protect her.

We stop at the sound of coywolves yipping in the distance. Heart appears terrified.

"We don't need to fear the animals nearly as much as we should fear people right now," I say, trying to allay her fears over the coywolves. I study the path in front of us in the growing light, being cautious thanks to the song of the dogs, which grow louder, indicating they are getting closer.

"What people?" she asks.

"All people, until we know otherwise."

"Where are we going?"

"To Karst."

I hope I am doing the right thing. There is no place else that has ever felt as safe. Besides, I want to look there for Gotham and Breanne, and to feel out the others, especially Suzanna, about their thoughts on this Resolution my father spoke of.

"The land of caves? It really exists?" She looks at me for the first time that day. I can't bear to look back at her, not wanting to see the contempt that has taken over her expression where I am concerned. "What is at Karst?"

"Hopefully Gotham and Breanne." I reach into the side pocket of my pack and pull out the two sets of eye shades. I hand the darker tinted ones to Heart.

She slips them on, then asks, "Your brother and sister?"

I welcome the questions. They feel better to me than the silence. But when I see people approaching along the rutted and cracking road, I must tell her to hush. I nod toward the group and slip on my own eye shades.

The family stops just ten feet from us, staring. The woman comes closer, reaches out and touches my hair. Then she reaches for Heart. I gently stop her from putting her hands on Heart.

"Please don't approach my cousin. She's been so traumatized—she can't stand to be touched, she has quit speaking as well."

I imagine that the wild-eyed look Heart gives fits perfectly with the story I concoct.

"I'm so sorry," the woman addresses me. "Where were you held?"

"ND3," I answer.

"Oh, so you might have word of my sister," the man says. "She was called Reba Truman."

"I am sorry that I do not have word for you. So much of my time was in isolation." I bow. "Please excuse us, we must go on."

"Yes, yes of course." The man pounds his chest and says, "Resist!"

"Resist," I respond in turn. I wonder if from now on I will question the level of loyalty to the Resisters with every person we come upon. Do these people know about the Resolution? Are they so fearful that they would go along with such a deplorable action?

When we come to a thick strand of hardwoods, I halt our progress.

"We should rest now and travel again at nightfall."

"Is something wrong? What has changed?"

"It's fine. It's just safer this way." I busy myself with setting up camp, trying to tamp down the fear building in my gut. I will do whatever it takes to keep Heart safe, even though she is obviously disgusted by the mere thought of me.

I pull some bread and cheese from the pack I've been carrying and set it out. Heart reaches for her canteen as I offer her an apple and my hand touches hers. She pulls away so quickly that I feel as if I've been kicked in the gut. I busy myself with checking over our supplies so I can hide the heightened color I am sure has found my cheeks.

We sleep under cover of the trees while the sun heats up the air outside the dome of the leafy canopy. I go to great lengths to be sure I don't touch Heart in any way.

I am awakened by the sound of hooves on the hard ground. Our supplies spread out from behind the boulder that otherwise hides us from view. This is not good. Heart sleeps between me and the errant supplies. I climb half over her in an effort to peer around the edge of the boulder to see who approaches.

Heart awakens, startled, and I am forced to place my hand over her mouth to quiet her. She bucks her body upward and I lower my full weight onto her. I look down into eyes the color of copper and I find myself wishing my mouth covered hers instead of my hand. I snap out of it.

"Quiet. There is danger," I whisper.

She stills long enough that I am comfortable removing my hand from over her mouth. I climb the rest of the way over her and pull our supplies farther behind the boulder.

I go back to Heart's side and we remain still. I gather from the amount of horse sounds that there are three of them. I can barely make out the words spoken.

"The general wants them back."

"There is no way they came in this direction. Let's double back."

I recognize the second voice as belonging to Jonas. The hoof sounds move farther away, but I am not convinced it is safe yet. We stay still and quiet for so long that the ground begins hurting my hip. I get up and crouch behind the boulder, stealing glances over it several times.

"They have come after us?" she whispers her question.

"Do not worry," I mutter.

After the sun dips lower in the sky, we gather our gear. I reach to help Heart reposition her pack when the glare she levels at me stops me cold. I hide the pain it inflicts on me but on the inside I am screaming at her to stop looking at me in such a disheartening way.

That is the way of the next several hours, me almost touching her accidentally and her recoiling in disgust. I do not know how long I will be able to hide how much this hurts me.

†

We are at a pivotal point in our journey as we are about to veer to the northeast. I walk to the edge of the ridge at Mt. Sanders, where the sun rises up over the horizon, a world away. In the distance opposite me is the ridge I'd stood on so long ago, right before being captured by Anointed soldiers. Below, the valley stretches out in a sweeping expanse of greens and yellows. In the middle of the vista sits ND3, east of the hemp and corn crops and west of the road that leads to the mines, and eventually the nuclear waste sites.

"Come stand up here with me," I say.

Heart approaches and I reach out to give her a hand up. She steps back.

"I am capable of doing this without assistance."

I cross my arms over my chest, and stare down into the valley where ND3 sits, the low buildings appearing to squat in the heat. Anger slowly replaces the pain Heart's unkind words and caustic looks have inflicted on me.

"Why do we stop?" she asks.

I stare at her for several icy moments before speaking.

"You're so miserable with me. Go—go back to 'what you know.'" I point at the trail that leads down the ridge to the detention center. From this direction it is only a moderate hike down from the ridge to the prison.

Heart freezes. She looks panicked but I am so very tired of trying to make her feel more relaxed, safer.

"What are you waiting for?" I ask. I point again down to ND3. "Go sit in a cell with *your people*. Or work in the fields or bird coops or mines with them…*your people*."

She stares, her eyes wide.

"Go, now! Go to your people. Be imprisoned with your people. I would never touch you intimately without your consent, but I can't say that about the rest of *my* people, the ones in power at the prisons, now that the roles are reversed."

Heart begins shaking. I start to tremble as well. The thought that she would call my bluff and leave to return to ND3 terrifies me.

"What's it going to be?" My voice is shredded.

She sobs.

"I don't expect you to be my concubine or my servant, but I do expect you to treat me with the same respect I do you. If you can't promise that, then please, just go. Go back to your people because I am done being looked at like a leper." It is taking every ounce of control I have to keep from crying.

Tears roll down Heart's face. I turn and stare off at the horizon, hoping the tears that are forming in my eyes are not visible.

"I will stay."

"What?" I ask. "Please repeat that louder."

"I would like to stay with you."

"Fine. If I accidentally touch you, please take care to hide your disgust from now on." I take a deep breath. "Okay, then we better get going. We have a lot of ground to cover. We will continue on for a couple more hours, and then we'll try to bunk down for the majority of the remaining daylight time."

I lead the way from the ridge, back on the path that will eventually bring us to Karst.

I am careful not to touch Heart, but when I fail and my hand brushes hers, she succeeds in better hiding her disgust. I am sad that an ultimatum was necessary, but I could not take the harshness of her response to me any longer.

We are careful with each other for the rest of the journey to Karst.

PART THREE: KARST

CHAPTER SEVEN

Two heavily armed guards meet us at the entrance to the cave.

"Don't be afraid," I tell Heart. "These are the good guys."

Heart looks at the guns. "Good to know."

"Kai! You have returned!" Jackson says as he approaches me.

I open my arms to receive an embrace from the tall, lean man when Andre grabs Jackson by the arm.

"You know better than to touch her before she has seen Dr. Bradshaw."

"Sorry. I am just so glad to see you," he says as he stands before me with a huge smile. "We were worried when we heard you'd not been in touch with anyone for so long."

"Jackson, it is wonderful to see you. And you as well, Andre."

Andre nods, then asks, "Who are you with?"

Heart stares openly at Andre, and I am pretty sure his compact and muscular body is daunting to her.

"I have brought a guest. Is the doctor available to see us now? I am so anxious to see Suzanna and to introduce her to Rachel."

I bounce slightly on my toes in anticipation. I hope the reception we receive will not be a disappointment. The Council may oversee the practical challenges of living in a network of caves and caverns, but Suzanna rules the forces of the heart and soul, and to me that is where I will find the most comfort right now.

"I will check on the doctor's availability to see you," Andre says. He turns to Jackson. "I trust you'll contain your excitement to see Kai until her exam is done?"

He doesn't give Jackson the chance to answer him before he marches away.

"He's still a wee bit uptight?" I tease. Jackson and I laugh.

"Some things never change," Jackson responds.

Only moments later, Andre reappears.

"Dr. Bradshaw will see you now."

We follow Andre down the south tunnel until the rough, brown walls open into a larger cavern. I remember the first time I stepped into the shiny, white-walled area. I'd never seen anything like it and had spun around looking in all directions. I look at Heart and she shows the same look of wonder I must have shown my first time here.

Andre shows us to separate examination rooms. I nod for Heart to go inside her room.

"It is an easy exam. It's just to keep us from introducing new sickness to the population of Karst. They will take your vitals, look in your eyes and throat, and draw some blood to check for the Trypto Krouse parasite."

Heart goes into the room and Andre closes the door. He then gestures toward the room next to it and I enter.

I undress and slip on the gown left on the stainless steel countertop. I sit on the edge of the table when the doctor comes in. I smile.

"I am so happy to see you," I say.

Dr. Bradshaw's smile is barely visible beneath the mask and face shield she wears. Her hair beneath the ties for the mask and shield is disheveled and I know she rushed to get prepped to see us. She has also donned latex gloves up to her elbows.

"You know how much I adore your attire," I tease.

"And you know how much I can't wait to clear you so I can take all this off and say hello with some manners."

"Then let's get this done." I open my arms. "See, all my body parts are here."

Dr. Bradshaw laughs. She grabs the cart with the instrument tray and stands close to me, then she shines the light in my eyes, moving it left to right and back again.

"Open wide," she instructs.

I do as I'm told. The doctor looks in my mouth, then my ears. She starts palpating my neck, moving my joints, and I am diligent about not letting on when the prodding causes pain.

Dr. Bradshaw stands in front of me, studying my face for a long time.

"What?" I finally ask, already knowing why she stares.

"This is new." The doctor traces the scar above my left eyebrow.

"It's nothing."

"Where have you been, Kai?"

"ND3."

"A detention center?"

"Yes. But not for too long."

She removes the gown from my shoulders and starts pressing around that area. I flinch.

"Where else were you hurt, other than your face and shoulder?"

"Nowhere else." I don't look at her when I lie. I study the white walls.

"This burn?" the doctor asks as she holds up my hand.

"It's nothing." I pull my hand away. "Are we almost done?"

"I'd like to do a gynecological exam on you."

"What? You've never done that before."

"It'll be quick."

"Why are you doing this to me?" Tears well up in my eyes. I don't want Dr. Bradshaw to see what still causes me so much pain deep inside. Then I am bothered by another thought. "Will you be doing the same to Rachel? She's probably so scared right now."

"Should I examine her that way?"

I square my shoulders.

"I don't know." And I don't. I don't know anything about Rachel Hart's life prior to locking eyes with her across the room at ND3 that first time. "I don't think so. But I can't be sure. Why are you doing this to me?"

"Come on, Kai. You know how important these health screenings are."

I do know the importance. But this was so much more invasive. I stare at the doctor. "Okay," I finally agree.

Dr. Bradshaw has me get prone on the table and begins her examination by palpating the areas where my thighs meet my groin. I know the exact moment the doctor finds the cigarette burns there. Tears burn my eyes as I think back to the horrible day I was assaulted.

I squeeze my eyes shut, forcing the tears out, as Dr. Bradshaw does the internal examination.

Afterward, she draws some blood and gives me some clean clothes to change into. "Get dressed and then we'll talk."

I do so, then the doctor returns. She sits across the small table from me.

"I'm concerned about the amount of scarring on your vaginal wall."

I don't look at her. I can't bear to know that she knows how I've been defiled.

"I'm signing off on your entry form, pending your blood work, but I'm also recommending that you see a therapist."

"There's nothing wrong with me. I don't need therapy."

"I remember the first time Gotham and Breanne brought you here. You were so young. And sweet."

"And now I'm neither." I wonder if Dr. Bradshaw is discouraged by the person I've become over the years.

"You were the first child I'd ever drawn blood from who didn't cry."

"I was stubborn like that. I was so happy that the twins trusted me enough to bring me with them that there was no way I was going to make them wish they'd left me at the homestead."

"You didn't have to be so stoic then, and you don't have to be now." Dr. Bradshaw sighs. She gives my hand a light, reassuring squeeze. "Laura will show you to your temporary quarters. I will do Rachel's exam now."

"Please take extra care with her. She's so out of sorts right now. I hope this isn't overwhelming for her." I look away, not wanting Dr. Bradshaw to see how much caring is in my eyes.

"I will be very careful and gentle with her."

I nod, then follow Laura to my temporary room. Laura explains that the interior door leads to the room Heart will be in after her exam, while she also awaits her clearance.

Once left alone, I pace the room waiting for Heart. I still feel pain from the exam but cannot dwell on that.

When I hear voices in the hallway I go to the door but when I open it, Heart is already in her room. I go to the interior door and lean my forehead against it. I think of how Heart had held me when I had my shoulder put back into its socket. Her touch had meant so much to me then. I fight against the longing to feel her touch again.

"Kai?" Heart asks through the door.

"Yes, I am here."

The doorknob turns and I take a step back.

"Thank you for putting my mind at ease before the exam. Dr. Bradshaw is wonderful."

"You didn't find the exam to be too invasive?" I smile.

"No, it was just as you said—vitals, a quick exam, and then blood drawn."

"Good. I'm glad it wasn't too hard for you." I am relieved that the doctor has not thought an internal exam was necessary for her.

"Dr. Bradshaw gave me something for my headache. She said it's probably the altitude and that I should also drink plenty of water."

I am sad that I am just now hearing that Heart has been uncomfortable.

"I will rest now while I can."

"Yes, that is wise. Rest well," I say.

Heart closes the door between us.

I try to sleep, but all I can do is worry about the results of the tests. What would I do if I found out I am infected with something and can't stay at Karst? What if Heart is a carrier of something? I know that if Heart isn't allowed to stay I will leave with her. But I do not know what she will decide should the results be against me staying.

†

Soon, we are cleared to integrate into life at Karst. We enter the lounge area and I embrace Suzanna. Twice I try to pull away from the woman with the long, gray hair, but Suzanna holds on to me for a long time. Finally we break from the embrace.

"My dearest Kai, we feared the worse when Gotham told us you'd disappeared while delivering a message for your father."

Suzanna takes my still shorn head into her hands. I place my hands over hers.

"It is all fine now. I promise," I say.

Suzanna kisses my forehead. The gesture makes me want to cry, so I pull away farther, squeeze Suzanna's shoulder, and then glance around.

"Where are Gotham and Breanne?"

"I am sorry, child, they moved on weeks ago." She turns to Heart. "And who have we here?"

"Suzanna, let me introduce you to Rachel Prince, my traveling companion." I see the recognition on Suzanna's face when she hears the last name I have chosen for Rachel. I had gone through a stage when I was young where I made everyone at Karst call me Prince Kai. They were all overly accommodating to my young self.

"Welcome, Rachel." Suzanna takes both of Heart's hands in hers and smiles. She cocks her head and looks deeply into Heart's eyes. "You can rest assured that you will be safe here with us."

"Thank you," Heart whispers. She stares at a large marble statue of one of Suzanna's goddesses in the corner, then sinks into the background as I pepper Suzanna with questions of my siblings.

"They were mostly well when they departed, albeit very worried for you."

The three of us turn as a young man enters.

"Kai, my friend!"

"Dawson! How wonderful to see you." I smile and embrace him. I pull away and study him. His beard stubble is dark but sparse, and he appears to have gained a little weight, which looks good on him. "As handsome as ever. Where is Heidi?"

"She is in bed."

"She's sick?"

"No, preparing to birth."

"Oh, that's wonderful," I exclaim, the love in my heart suddenly threatening to overpower me. Winthrop Brodie might be my blood, but the citizens of Karst are my true people. I look at Suzanna who is now openly studying Heart.

"Kai, dear, why don't you go with Dawson to wish Heidi well? I will entertain Rachel while you are gone," Suzanna says.

Dawson and I both turn to Heart. Dawson looks quickly at me, then at Suzanna, who nods her head to the right.

"Heidi will be so happy to see you." Dawson smiles.

I glance back at Heart as I leave with him.

At Heidi and Dawson's quarters, I throw my arms around my friend. I cannot believe how amazing Heidi looks. She glows!

"I've been so worried about you." Heidi cries when we finish our hug.

"I am fine." I open my arms wide, ignoring the pain in my shoulder. "See?"

"Your hair leaves a little to be desired," Heidi teases.

"What? I'm looking to start a new style. Besides, it's so easy to care for." I can't stop smiling. Heidi's light brown hair has grown out, hanging down her back, and her skin seems lighter than usual, probably from time spent in bed instead of outdoors. She is pale, but not "anointed pale" as some would tease.

"I knew our coyote would return," Heidi says.

"Yes, always the coyote. I met a couple of Dawson's rodent relatives lately." I wink at Heidi.

"I'm feeling a lot like the elephant Suzanna says I am animal mates with." Heidi gestures at her bulging midsection.

I look at her and smile, knowing she must feel uncomfortable in her pregnancy.

"Dawson tells me you are traveling with a very attractive woman," Heidi says.

I feel the blush growing on my cheeks.

"If she makes you happy, I am happy for you," Heidi says.

"Tell me about the baby. Do you hope for a boy or a girl? When will you give birth?" I ask, effectively changing the subject.

†

I slow as I approach Suzanna and Heart. I know it is not right for me to eavesdrop, but I cannot help myself. It is not lost on me that this is the first time since leaving ND3 that Heart is not under my control.

The women sit at a low table, on cushions opposite each other.

"We will dine later. Can I get you anything in the meantime?" Suzanna asks. "Perhaps a chicory beverage?"

"No, thank you," Heart answers.

"From where do you know our Kai?" Suzanna interlaces her fingers and rests her hands in her lap.

I remain silent; wanting to hear what will come next, but also terrified of what might be said.

I watch as Heart looks down at her own hands. I had noticed earlier that the top part of her hands have turned red in patches where the sleeves of her shirt have left the sensitive skin to burn in the sun.

"Do not be afraid. You are safe here," Suzanna says.

"ND3," Heart whispers.

"The prison?"

"Yes, ma'am."

"For how long were you incarcerated together?" Suzanna asks.

I hold my breath. Would she tell Suzanna that she was once my imprisoner—one of the group who tormented me?

"We weren't incarcerated together."

I feel something resembling relief wash over me and don't understand the feeling.

Suzanna is quiet for a long time, and then she asks, "You are Anointed?"

"Yes." Heart hesitates for only a second.

Suzanna reaches across the table and takes Heart's hands in hers.

"You are still safe here, child."

I feel the sting of tears in my eyes. *Do not cry, please do not cry.* I so love Suzanna and her way with all people.

"Here at Karst we do not care from where you come, only to where you are going. As all of us do, feel free to pray or worship, but only in the privacy of your quarters. We do not prohibit it, but we do ask that you respect the comfort of others by not referring to your God in any way in public."

Heart nods.

I try to recall if I ever knew of Heart to worship in any way. Only once did she make a reference to praying that I can recall.

"You will be quartered with Kai so you must work out an understanding with her about your faith expression, as I assume you already have."

I don't want to give Heart the chance to tell Suzanna how much she is disgusted by me, our situation, or my mere presence. I clear my throat as I enter the room from the shadows of the corridor.

"All is well?" I smile at Suzanna, and then look at Heart.

"All is well," Suzanna responds.

Several young people join us.

"We want to hear how it was to turn the tide on the oppressors," one of the young men states.

"Yes, how dreadful was it to be imprisoned, and how karmic to become the free-living again?" a pretty young woman asks me.

"It was dreadful, but now it is in the past," I say, glancing at Heart as I speak.

"Did you get scanned when you were freed?" Dawson, who has just now rejoined us, asks.

"Yes," I answer. I wonder if anyone at Karst has heard about the transmittal of the scanned data. I glance at Heart, but don't hold her gaze. "It has been a long day—hell, a long few months—if it pleases all, I would like a rest before dinner."

Suzanna stands.

"Yes, a rest. All of you young people move along. There will be plenty of time to discuss the future with Kai after she and Rachel rest and we have dinner."

At the mention of Rachel, all eyes are on her. I can see the blush creep up her neck and across her cheeks. The others had been sneaking glances at Heart up to this point, but it seems having her name spoken gives them permission to openly stare at her.

Rachel. I silently taste her name on my lips and wonder if I will ever really get used to it.

Once the three of us are alone again, Suzanna has both of us sit at the table with her.

"Before you take your rest, tell me about the tattoo scans," Suzanna says.

"I was already in the system, so they just updated my data. Rachel wasn't in the system and has no identifying paperwork. She is registered to me." My voice is low, and I know Heart must think that is because I'm embarrassed to say these words. "It was necessary for her safety."

"I see," Suzanna says to me. Then she turns to address Heart. "We are able to remove the UV tattoos safely."

I watch Heart, gauging her reaction. When she says nothing, I clear my throat.

"Whatever Rachel wants to do, is fine with me."

Suzanna takes Heart's hand.

"Keeping your tattoo gives you Kai's continued protection. Removing it gives you, well, freedom, until that is taken away again. It's not much more than just permanently neutralizing the UV ink. It doesn't hurt and won't scar." Suzanna squeezes her hand. "Come with me, darling. Let's go talk and we can remove your tattoo if that's what you choose."

"I will go to quarters. Will I be at my usual?" I ask.

"Yes, you will be quartered there with Rachel."

"Thank you. For everything." I nod, then give Suzanna a slight bow.

After Suzanna and Heart leave the room, I head to my quarters. I am only bathed and settled in for a few minutes when I hear the tapping on the door.

"Come in."

Heart slowly opens the door and enters the room, not looking at me.

"Oh." I blink, confused by her presence so soon. "That was fast."

I don't know if the quick timing means Heart has chosen to remain marked as my property. I try to see if there is any sign of work done to her shoulder without her knowing that is what I am doing.

"I have bathed. Would you like me to show you to the facility before you lie down to rest?" I ask her.

"If it's no trouble."

"Come, through this door. Here is clean clothing for you as well." I hand the clothing to her and lead her down the shiny, white corridor to the west-side bathing room.

Heart looks around the large room. I wonder if the memory of the showers at ND3 is assaulting her mind as they did mine when I first entered for my own shower. I wonder for how long I will have to fight hard against the images of women being sprayed down, open to the guards' scrutiny, lust, and ridicule.

I gesture toward the last shower stall, nod toward the heavy stone door. "The end one has the best spray of warm water."

Heart stands still for so long I grow worried. I go to her side, and reach for her arm. She pulls just out of my reach and I flinch at the movement.

"I am capable of figuring out the bathing facility," she says.

"As you wish," I whisper. "You will have privacy in the facility this time of day." I hurry back to the sleeping quarters, feeling the burn of Heart's continued rejection.

As I pace back and forth in my quarters, I know I won't be able to relax if I don't get what's bothering me off my chest. I hurriedly split the bedding in two and arrange the cushions and blankets into opposite corners of the room, then I seek out Suzanna.

I find my friend in the meditation room and feel guilty about disturbing her, but not guilty enough to withdraw.

"Kai, dear, I thought you were resting."

"I'm sorry to interrupt your quiet time," I say.

"Come here."

I go to Suzanna and she envelopes me in a warm embrace.

"Tell me what is upsetting you."

I tell her what I overheard at my homestead and how I fear genocide is looming.

"I can't stand the thought of something happening to Heart—to Rachel. What am I to do?" I feel the tears stinging my face and find my breath coming out in a ragged sob.

"My dear, dear child. It will be okay. We here at Karst will protect both you and Rachel with our very lives." She wipes away my tears. "You know that, right?"

I nod.

"Go rest now. We will discuss this more later," Suzanna says.

I take my leave and go back to my quarters. I have just begun to lounge on the cushions in my corner when Heart enters the room and goes to her own. She looks stunning in the soft, light-cotton pants and sleeveless top. Her beauty makes my chest ache. I roll over to face the wall.

I can hear her stretching out on the cushions and inhaling the fragrance from the blankets.

Maybe an hour later, just as I start to finally drift to sleep, a noise at the door awakens me. I jump up.

"You are requested to come dine at this time," a voice says through the door.

I stretch my shoulder.

"Does it still hurt?" Heart asks.

I stare at her for a moment, feeling somewhat confused by her sudden concern for me.

"Your shoulder—and other injuries—do they still bother you?"

"Sometimes," I say. "Particularly upon first rising. Let's not keep Suzanna and the others waiting."

At dinner, I introduce all the others to Rachel. Suzanna makes it clear she is welcomed at Karst for as long as she wishes to be there. Bronwyn, a five year old cutie with wild, dark curls and big brown eyes, is shy around Heart. I catch her watching Heart with a look of awe on her face. I wonder if it's the creamy paleness of Heart's skin, or the lightness of her now golden-amber eyes that have captured Bronwyn's attention.

Emily, whom I've known since my first visit with the twins to Karst, enters the room. She grabs me and pulls me into a big hug. The action hurts my shoulder, and when I look over at Heart, she gives me a look that makes me think she has registered the pain in my expression. I pull away slightly from Emily and force a smile.

Emily cries, silent tears that stab at my chest. Her hands clutch at my head, feeling the scalp where my hair has begun to come back in. Her full lower lip trembles.

"I was so afraid for you."

"I'm here, I'm fine." I maintain eye contact for only a moment before looking away from her intense scrutiny.

Dr. Bradshaw eyes me from across the room, watching me for signs of needing therapy, I am sure. Her hair is neatly combed, and I see less pepper and more salt in the mix now. I smile at her, hoping to alleviate her fear for my mental well-being.

"It's so good to have you here," Emily says, more composed, drawing my attention back to her. She embraces me again and I feel her tremble. "I was so worried."

"Really, I'm fine. It's good to be here," I say.

Emily looks over my shoulder and I am sure she is checking out Heart.

"Sit," I say. "Tell me how you've been."

"I've been good, but am better now that I know you are safe." She reaches to my face and touches the scar above my left eye. I feel my face heating up as I think of the last time I saw Emily, when she kissed me and made me feel tingly. At one time, Emily's touch to my face would have sent a shiver through my entire body. Now it feels sweet, but awkward.

"They hurt your beautiful face."

I can feel Heart's eyes on me but don't look at her. I don't want Heart to look in my eyes and know that I'd give anything for her to touch me the way Emily is now.

Suzanna sets a large platter of grilled vegetables on the table. I have missed the variety of foods from the large fields beyond the mountain harboring Karst. I am happy for the distraction as we all go to the table and take our seats, where Heart sits on one side of me, and Emily on the other.

Heart is studying the contents of her fork. It takes only a moment for me to realize why she hesitates. The garden at ND3 grew green beans, tomatoes, and cucumbers, all mostly for the Anointed's consumption.

"That is sure to be the tastiest zucchini you've ever had," I say.

Her lip twitches briefly as if hiding a smile before she puts the squash in her mouth. She nods her satisfaction. Then she holds up her fork again.

"And this will be the best as well?"

"Oh yes, that will be the best Brussels sprout you've ever eaten." I force my gaze off her mouth then, and to her eyes. The speckled, radiant amber I find there makes my insides swirl.

Emily scoots closer to me. There is a subtle shift during dinner, and I am amused that Heart's hand accidentally touches mine once during our meal. I am pretty sure Heart is a little jealous of Emily's attention toward me. I can't deny how much I like this thought.

I feel a little ashamed that I am enjoying the company of all these great people while the turmoil over what I've heard about the Resolution roils inside me. As if reading my mind, Suzanna gives me a little smile and wink from across the table. I know I can trust her with the information I gave her earlier, and that she will guide me.

As the meal winds down, Dawson stands.

"Kai, will you come meet with me and some of the council?"

I look from Suzanna to Heart.

"Go, take care of business. I will entertain Rachel," Suzanna says.

I smile at Suzanna, but do not chance a look at Heart before leaving with Dawson.

†

Dawson and I enter the Council Chamber where several people, including Jackson, already sit on cushions around a low table. The very dark man I know as Shelton stands and bows toward me.

"Welcome back to Karst, Kai."

I bow slightly at the head of the council. "Thank you," I say as the others stand.

Patricia comes to me and gives me a quick, but warm hug.

"Welcome back. We are so glad you are safe." She pulls back from me and gives me a studied look. I take stock of her as well, her medium brown hair and eyes looking warm and friendly.

"Thank you," I respond. I am pleased to see that Patricia still sits on the council.

I am then introduced to Carlos and Nell, two people I knew previously only by sight. We shake hands and then Jackson hugs me before suggesting we get started. Shelton speaks first.

"The Resisters have changed. General Grayson is no longer considered our ally."

My head snaps up. "What is that all about?"

"General Grayson is keen on genetic work to help the Resisters against the Anointed, not in finding peace between the two." He watches me with his black eyes. "He has gathered about him some like-minded people, and some misguided ones as well."

"I have heard they are now able to transmit the information from the chip readers to a computer under Grayson's control. Has anyone heard of that?" I ask the group.

"Yes," Patricia answers. "We have heard rumors of that, and so much more. It is the general's son, Sergeant Thomas Grayson, who is in charge of the technology they are using."

"Gotham and Breanne have gone on a reconnaissance mission to try to determine General Grayson's next move," Shelton adds. "We need to find out how far along he is with his objective, and then successfully thwart it if the Peace Movement is to thrive."

I am distracted by thoughts of my siblings, and hope the twins are safe. I had so wanted to see them when I arrived at

Karst. The words I'd almost missed echo in my brain. *The Peace Movement*. What is this movement? I don't want to ask so as not to have to admit I don't know what my siblings have been up to. "I've been gone a long time. What is the current status of the movement?"

Shelton and Carlos exchange glances. Patricia starts to speak, but Shelton interrupts her. "Your siblings will tell you all about it. You do plan to follow after them?"

"Yes, that is my intention."

"Now we need to discuss something else," Jackson says, looking at me. "Suzanna tells me that Kai has something to share with us."

I look around at the others. I am nervous but know I must share this with them. I tell them the story of overhearing about the Resolution to exterminate all of the Anointed.

Nell gasps.

"I thought as much was coming, but hearing of it like this is quite disturbing," Shelton says.

"Disturbing, but not surprising." Jackson crosses his arms over his chest.

"Is there concurrence between your father and General Grayson?" Carlos asks.

"It appears so," I answer. "General Brodie seems to have taken a more hard-lined stance however. He believes Grayson will fall in line with his plans."

Of course I am disgusted that the order is coming from my own flesh and blood. I glance around and try to read the expressions on the faces before me. Do they trust me? Do they know I am as devastated by the plan as they are?

"Kai?"

"Pardon me?"

"I said you don't look well. No offense," Carlos says.

"None taken. I am just tired." I force a smile. "I am so very happy to be here with you all, but I am also anxious to join Gotham and Breanne."

We break for the evening after agreeing to meet for strategizing the next day.

As we leave the meeting area, everyone is going in different directions, but Dawson walks with me for several moments.

"You are accepted as one of us, you know that, right?"

"Thank you, my friend." Squeezing his hand, I smile and nod my head.

We separate and I return to the main lounge area. I stand in the doorway and watch as Heart is entertained by some storytellers. She looks over to me and I nod my approval. I look to my right where Emily sits, watching me.

I scan the rest of the people in the large room. A young man in the back of the room, Scotty, softly plays a flute. One of the many things I love about Karst is the assortment of artists, musicians, storytellers, and philosophers. The creators, the questioners, are not embraced by the Anointed as they were historically by the Resistance, whether they are Christian or not. One such storyteller, an elder named Stella, is testifying now.

"They were led by what was called a President back then," she adds to what she'd been saying.

"No way. One government ruled over all of this?" The preteen girl named Pasha spreads her arms wide, indicating the world outside of this cavernous safe haven. "How could that be?"

The old woman leans closer to the fire.

"That was a very long time ago. They called it Democracy and it worked for just over 240 years."

"Wow," Pasha says. "The whole world ruled by one person!"

"Not quite." Stella laughs. "There were parts of the world far, far away that weren't a part of the big government. They had their own governments and their own problems."

"The biggest problems were the religious people. Now they are the Anointed." Pasha crosses her arms over her chest as she says this.

"Hush, now," Freda says from beside me. She glances at Heart as she speaks. "No need to place blame."

I watch Freda, and think about when I was younger and would sit in this very room, listening to the old women's stories. That was before I understood that the world's problems were about more than the oppression of the Resisters by the Anointed.

"What happened?" someone asks.

"When the Christians' hatred of others became greater than their love of their god, it all fell apart," Suzanna says.

I watch Heart for a reaction, but her expression is guarded.

"So it's the Christians' fault," Pasha says.

"It wasn't just them, but they were the worst." Freda looks across the cavern at Heart. "It was also the Muslims and Jews. Everyone who thought their way was the only way was at fault."

"Everyone except pagans!" the girl sings out.

"Pagans were no better. They didn't work hard enough for peace," Freda says.

"But soon our people will make peace and everything will be all right again."

"That's the plan, child, that's the plan," Suzanna says, her voice barely over a whisper.

My favorite storyteller is Suzanna; her voice is so smooth it feels like a caress. I lean closer to her, expecting her to say more, but she does not.

It is Emily who speaks next.

"Kai, would you like to testify?"

"No, thank you. I do not wish to tell a story today." I am grateful then when the group's attention goes back to Stella.

Dr. Bradshaw makes her way closer and stands near me.

"How are you, dear?"

"I am well." I give her my best smile. "Please do not be concerned for me."

"Have you been in pain?"

"Nothing I cannot handle." I squeeze her hand. "I am fine."

"Okay. Let me know if you need anything, even if it's just to talk."

"Thank you." I get a slight lump in my throat, but swallow past it. I am sincere and believe she knows this.

I say goodnight, then walk with Heart toward our quarters. I am still wondering about this Peace Movement when she pauses in the corridor and touches the shiny, smooth wall.

"Aren't you afraid we'll be crushed?" Heart asks as she looks up to the ceiling.

"I'd rather be crushed by the mountain I love than killed by the people who hate me." I am immediately sorry for the fear I have put in her eyes. I soften my voice. "No, I am not afraid of being crushed by the mountain. The walls in here are very strong."

"Why are they white?"

"Kaolin." I glance to the end of the corridor when I hear noise. Emily is standing there, staring at us. "I can tell you more about that later. Let's go inside our quarters now."

CHAPTER EIGHT

The next morning, alone with Heart in our quarters, I notice she is somber. She looks everywhere but at me, and I fear what little headway we've made softening her stance toward me is slipping.

I pass the time by knotting and weaving strings of hemp with crystal chips that Freda has given me. The one I am just completing has amber crystals that look like Heart's eyes in the sunshine.

"Would you like this?" I feel shy as I offer her the bracelet, holding it out to her.

She glances up and shrugs. When she doesn't reach for it I withdraw my hand.

I've become so weary with the constant effort to not touch her, even in the most platonic of ways. I want to withdraw, shield myself from the feelings I struggle to contain. At times, my energy lags, something I've never experienced before.

I am free, I will soon be leaving to join Gotham and Breanne, I have a real purpose again—and yet—I feel so tired and sad and overwhelmed.

"Kai."

I glance at Heart.

"I need you to explain something to me."

"I will try. What do you want to know?"

"I've been wondering. Ever since the processing center, you've quit really looking me in the eye. Since that day on the ridge, I have really been trying to treat you with more respect. But still, here, you look everyone in the eye but me."

"And?" I ask, feeling defensive.

"Why?"

I take a deep breath. I don't want to have this conversation, but I imagine it is time.

"It isn't safe to look at you. Once we stepped out of ND3, it was my responsibility to keep you safe. Looking at you and swooning is not going to help anyone."

"Swooning?" she asks with a slight smile.

"Please don't ridicule me," I say.

"I am not." She cocks her head to see my face better. "Tell me about the way you used to look at me."

I don't respond. I go about starting a new bracelet, one I may give to Emily just because I know she will cherish it. I feel Heart's eyes on me. Finally, she grabs my arm and pulls me around to face her. I swallow hard and look into her eyes. My breathing quickens.

"That," she says, her own breathing growing labored. "*That* look. Please tell me about it."

I try to look away, but gentle fingertips on the side of my chin guide my face back in her direction.

"That expression," she says. "It's the same expression you had on your face the first time I saw you."

I stare at her for several moments before responding.

"Awe."

"What?"

"The first time I saw you I was in awe of the ways my body reacted to you. It's—it's done the same thing every day since then, is doing the same thing now. I'm sorry if it's upsetting to you. I didn't mean for it to be then, and I don't mean for it to be now."

"Tell me more about this reaction?" she asks in a low voice. Heart removes her fingertips from my face, but doesn't break our gaze.

I think of all the looks of disgust, all the coldness she has leveled at me since leaving ND3, and shake my head.

"You want me to strip away my defenses? I'm sorry, *Rachel*, you have not earned that right after the way you've treated me ever since we left ND3." I toss the bracelet with the amber crystals onto the floor by her feet and quietly walk out of the room.

I know where I am going as soon as I am in the long corridor.

Suzanna looks up as I enter the lounging room. "Dear, you look distraught."

"It's nothing." I sit opposite her.

"I have known you for so very long, Kai. You cannot tell me nothing is wrong when I know better."

"I'm sorry."

"I was about to go to the meditation room. Would you like to join me?"

I nod.

Suzanna stands and reaches out her hand. I take it and let her lead me to the quiet meditation room.

We stand in the middle of the room and Suzanna studies me. She looks so intently at me for so long that I just know she is deep in my thoughts. I am both troubled by and grateful for this.

"You truly are in crisis."

"Yes," I whisper as tears form in my eyes.

"It might help if I can look into your past lives. I can put myself in a place where the dreams are sure to be about you. Are you ready for that yet?"

I shake my head. I know Suzanna does not take past life dreaming lightly and is sincere and caring in her suggestion, but I am not interested.

"I am only concerned with this life. Sorry."

"No need to apologize." She kisses my forehead, then steps away. "Let's get you comfortable."

Suzanna has me change into a thin, cotton robe, then guides me to sit on the floor. I sit, cross-legged, with my eyes closed. I listen to her movements and know she lights candles and incense, moves about the room calling upon the Goddess and God in a low voice.

She kneels before me and runs her fingers through my slightly grown out hair. "O Goddess within; O God within; O Goddess of the Moon, Sea, and Earth; O God of the Forest and Mountains; I give to you thanks for the safe return of our Sister, Kai."

Her fingers are gentle on my face.

"Tell me what you are thinking about," Suzanna says.

"I am afraid."

"You are safe here."

"I'm not afraid for me. I am afraid for Gotham and Breanne—for Rachel—for all peaceful people. I am afraid that my father's army will do something heinous and I'll be helpless to stop it." My breath is ragged. "I am afraid of my heart breaking beyond repair."

She applies cedarwood oil to my face, massages it into my forehead. I feel my shoulders begin to relax. Suzanna takes the robe off my shoulders and for a moment I tense. She responds with a whispered, "O Goddess of the Universe; O God of the Earth; I pray that you Heal my sweet Kai; Quench her fires with love; Feed her Peace with Your Peace."

Again, I relax. She massages the oil into my shoulders, then my neck, down to my clavicles.

I do not recall the last time I breathed so deeply. Suzanna matches my breaths in and out and I relax further.

"O Goddess of the Moon; O God of the Mountains; Light the path for Kai; Protect her from all harm."

She moves behind me and her hands knead the muscles of my upper back.

"Let the stress go, Kai." Her voice is silk.

I take a deep breath.

"You are safe with us. You have found your tribe here with us."

I feel safe from the outside dangers here at Karst. But my heart still breaks and I still feel danger coming from within me. Tears course down my cheeks.

I open my eyes and see Heart's face in the small window in the middle of the door. We make eye contact and I hate that she can probably see my tears. I close my eyes momentarily and when I reopen them there is no one peering through the window. I am unsure if I imagined her there or not.

I sob and Suzanna embraces me from behind. "Let it out, child, let it out."

I cry for what feels like a very long time. I become exhausted and just want to sleep.

Suzanna places a cup of water to my lips and I drink. "Let's get you to bed. You can rest until the evening meal. Unless you want to go now for the midday meal?"

"I'd rather go rest." When I stand she offers her arm to steady me.

I leave wearing the robe and carrying my clothes. She sees me to my quarters and I am beyond relieved that Heart is not there.

I am prone under the soft sheet, facing the wall, when Heart enters our quarters. She gets something from her bedding and leaves again. I am thankful that she assumes I am sleeping and doesn't try to engage me. Ha! Like she would bother? Tears silently flow.

I stare at the glossy wall. It is soothing to look at. It is soothing to lie here and do absolutely nothing. I am so tired. I don't think I'll ever *not* be tired again.

Heart returns and tells me our evening meal is ready. I am hungry but cannot bear the idea of getting out of bed.

"Please tell Suzanna I will not be dining tonight," I whisper.

She leaves again.

Heart comes in several more times throughout the evening. Each time she stays only a moment and does not speak. Finally, at one such time I roll away from the wall to face her.

"What is it?" I say, my voice hoarse and raw.

"Are you not well?"

I don't answer. How do I? I become miserable in her gaze.

"I'm fine," I finally respond as tears come and I roll over to face the wall again. I stare at the stark, clean whiteness of it and my tears burn my eyes.

I feel Heart's hand on my back and it startles me at first. Then she is stretched out beside me, embracing me from behind, stroking my hair.

"What is it?" she asks.

I cannot answer, I just cry, feeling the heat of her against my back.

"Is this okay?" she asks.

"Yes."

She holds me for a long time. I sleep.

†

When I awaken in the morning, she is gone. I look to the opposite corner to where her bedding is and she is not there. My body longs for her. My soul yearns for her. But I am done crying.

I get up and gather my things for a shower. I will wash away the oil and go eat. Then I will prepare myself for whatever I need to do to get things moving in the direction of leaving to find Gotham and Breanne.

I am finished bathing and feel so much better in a fresh set of clothes. I am ravenous and make my way to the dining area.

Emily intercepts me.

"I miss you."

"I am right here," I respond.

125

"That's not what I mean." She touches my face. "Suzanna acts as if you and Rachel are coupled, yet I see no intimacy and you do not look happy."

"I am fortunate to be free, and to be here at Karst," I say, choosing my words carefully.

"We can pick up where we left off," Emily says as she moves closer.

I think about our one kiss, about how I would have done anything with her—for her—had she asked back then. So much has changed.

"No, we cannot." I look away.

"Tell me you love her and I will not pursue this any further."

Now I look her squarely in the eyes. "I love Rachel."

"Then so be it. I wish you much luck and happiness." Emily sighs.

I stand still until Emily is around the corner of the long corridor. I bring my fingertips to my lips. I cannot believe I have said those words out loud. I cannot believe how sweet her name felt on my lips. I swallow hard.

When I make it to the dining area, Freda and Pasha are there enjoying some blackberries and honey-sweetened water. The others have already finished the morning meal, it appears.

"Good morning! We missed you at dinner last night," Freda says as she studies my face.

"Good morning."

"I was just going to make some tea and toast. Shall I make some for you as well?"

"If it's no trouble," I answer Freda.

"Wood sorrel tea?" Freda asks and I nod. I know the tea will help with the sourness lingering in my stomach from not eating last night.

Pasha is staring at me. She continues to do so until Freda places the toast and tea onto the table and nudges her.

Freda smiles at me and offers honey for the toast. I spread a thin layer and hand it back to her.

"Is Suzanna around this morning?"

"She's with a group in the meditation room." Freda watches me. "Rachel has gone to worship with the progressives this morning."

I am surprised. Yet I'm not, either. I am glad that the Progressive Christians have reached out to Heart. I hope it is a good thing for her.

Suzanna enters the dining area and I smile at her.

"How are you today, Kai?"

"I am good," I answer.

She kisses the top of my head before sitting across from me.

Freda and Pasha finish eating and take leave of us.

"I was worried for you." Suzanna squeezes my hand briefly.

"I am fine now."

"Rachel was very concerned."

I nod. I think about Rachel holding me last night and feel conflicted. I know it was just that she had pity for me, and I don't plan to ever give her reason to feel that again.

Suzanna takes a deep breath and settles herself physically in the way she does when she's unsettled mentally. Usually she becomes so only when dreams haunt her.

I continue to watch her. I know without her saying that she dreamt of me after we last spoke. I also know she will offer to tell me the story in her dream. She always offers—that is her way.

She closes her eyes momentarily. "Shall I talk about my dreams from last night?"

"No, thank you though." I bow my head briefly. "I mean no disrespect."

"Of that I am certain, love." Suzanna smiles at me just briefly. "In all the time I've known you, Rachel is the first person I've known you to couple with."

I sit in shocked silence. Does Suzanna not see the resentment and hatred in Heart's eyes when she looks at me? How could that be so? Even Emily sees the lack of intimacy between us.

"Yet even so," Suzanna continues, "There is obviously trouble between you two. I do hope you aren't meant to break each other's hearts. That would be such a pity."

My belly flutters again with the word "heart." I don't tell Suzanna that my heart is already broken.

We look up at a sound in the doorway. I wonder how much Heart has heard, but will never ask.

"I will go visit Heidi now if that's okay," I say.

"Yes, go see your friend." She turns to Heart. "Rachel, will you sit and visit with me?"

I give Suzanna a sidelong look.

"Don't worry, dear. There is so much we can discuss that isn't about you," Suzanna says, her tone teasing.

I take my leave, and within minutes I am knocking gently on the door to Heidi and Dawson's quarters. After only a few seconds, Dawson opens the door. He smiles at me and invites me in.

Heidi looks me over for several moments, eyes narrowed.

"You're too thin, still. I'm going to have to talk to Suzanna about making sure you are fattened up."

"Ah, it's good to be lean when you travel long distances." I don't say how much I would like to put on a few pounds before leaving again because I know there isn't enough time for that.

"I know you will eventually go, but it sure is nice knowing you are here and safe." Heidi reaches for my hand, then Dawson's. "It's so nice to have my two favorite people here at the same time."

I squeeze her hand.

"Dawson," Heidi gives him a sweet smile. "Can you let me have a moment alone with Kai?"

"Girl talk." He chuckles. He leaves the room with an exaggerated rolling of his eyes.

"Am I in trouble?" I only half-jokingly ask.

"I don't know. Should you be?"

"No, I have done nothing too egregious." I pretend to contemplate that.

"No, I'm sure you haven't. But I dare say you've broken Emily's heart."

I look away.

"The heart wants what the heart wants," Heidi says, making my belly quiver at the word *heart*.

"I do suppose you are right."

"If you're happy, I'm happy for you." She watches me intently.

I do not contradict her.

She gives me a shy smile and asks if I'll call Dawson back in. I do so happily.

Soon Heidi grows tired and Dawson tells her that he and I will go to a meeting with the council while she rests.

We enter the room at the same time as the others and it doesn't take long for order to take hold.

"Your twin siblings have something big planned, I just do not know what it is," Shelton states, turning to me. "I do hope it is something large and definitive, time is running out for bringing all the outliers together into the Peace Movement."

I feel the urgency in Shelton's words. The mention of this Peace Movement stirs something inside me. I hope it is exactly as it sounds, I hope Gotham and Breanne are indeed in the middle of this thing, and I hope they welcome me to it with open arms.

"There are so many hidden pockets of people who must come together to fight for peace if it is to be successful," Carlos says.

I listen carefully and wonder about the specific words being spoken. No one says *we* or *our*, there doesn't seem to be any ownership here of the movement.

"I want to leave soon to find my siblings." I will not be shy about my desire to own the necessary actions.

"Do you want company?" Jackson asks.

I smile at him. "Sure."

"Then we should prepare now," Shelton says.

We. Now we are getting somewhere.

"I will get a list of necessary supplies for our journey," Nell offers.

Dawson looks around the room at everyone before looking down at the ground. When the meeting breaks up, I stay behind to address my longtime friend.

"Dawson, it is important that we have some strong warriors stay behind to protect Karst. I will miss you terribly, but Heidi and Suzanna need you here."

"I know I must stay behind, and I will miss you, too. Tremendously."

After he steps away I linger a few moments longer, reflecting on my time incarcerated, when the only pleasure I had was my next glimpse of Heart. Now, I find pleasure in the people of Karst, the stories, the softness of it all, and the knowledge that Heart is safe, even if I now see in her eyes mostly contempt for me.

†

I walk toward our quarters with Heart and steal shy glances every now and then. Finally I ask about what is on my mind.

"What did you and Suzanna talk about while I was gone visiting Heidi and the others?"

"Suzanna told me about how very long ago a group of survivalists carved out the cave town and called it Jamestown. She said they feared the country was getting too dangerous and carved a safe haven out of the mountain."

I nodded. I had known that Karst was once called Jamestown, but no one talks about why they changed the name.

"And she told me about the white walls. About how Stanley James, a founder of Jamestown, was a lover of fine things and shipped white clay called kaolin from what once was the state of Georgia, to fire onto the walls, to make them aesthetically pleasing." She pauses. "That was just before the war broke out. Before the bombing changed everything."

"She did give you quite the history lesson," I say. "What else did you talk about?"

"She told me about the first time she came to Karst." She smiles. "And we talked about you, of course."

I spin around to look at her.

"I am teasing you."

I stare at her.

"What?" she asks.

"I don't think you've ever really done that—tease me."

"I don't suppose I have."

We arrive at our quarters and go inside. I want to ask her about her worship time but don't know how to broach the subject. Then she does it for me.

"I spent time this morning worshipping with the Progressives."

"How was that?" I smile, happy that I don't have to be the one to bring it up.

She looks away, appears shy.

"Was it a good experience for you? You don't have to go back if you don't want to."

"It's not that I don't want to go again. It was just very confusing for me."

"How so?" I want her to feel she can speak freely with me.

"They have an ancient Bible. An actual *book*. When they read from it, I did not recognize God's word."

No wonder she was confused. There is often discussion in Karst about the bastardization of the Christian readings that was done by the racists who hijacked the religion long ago. "Did you like the words though?"

"I did, very much so. I also love how joyous the Progressives are. And I like how their music and hymns are… softer." She smiles now. "I've noticed that everything is softer here—the music, the fabric, the energy."

I smile, agreeing wholeheartedly.

"There was a kind energy in worship today. I asked Sister Nanette if that is always the case and she said yes. She described it as *touchy-feely*," Heart says.

"The Anointed aren't touchy-feely, I take it?"

"No, not at all."

"So." Feeling a new connection with her, I ask what I'd wanted to for a long time. "What did a Day of Atonement look like in ND3?"

"Day of Atonement?"

"You know, when we weren't allowed out of our cells so you could atone for your treatment of us."

"Prayer Day. We called it Prayer Day."

She looks away now and I feel horrible. Why did I not think before I spoke?

We are quiet for a long time before she speaks again.

"Since Dawson and Heidi are awaiting a baby, I take it only some people here are non-breeders?"

I chuckle, then see her unease and feel bad for doing so.

"Yes, that is correct." I look at her and her nervousness is palatable. "Are you in need of supplies?" I ask, as vaguely as I can.

"Yes," she whispers. "Soon."

"I will see that you get whatever you need," I say. I feel bad that I hadn't thought of her needs before this moment.

"Thank you," she says.

I think about her advice to me when I was in ISO at ND3, about acting like a breeder, and can't believe how far away those circumstances feel to me in distance and time now.

As if knowing where my thoughts have gone, she speaks in a low voice.

"The first time I saw you, I wanted to protect you."

I let the words sit between us for a long time before responding.

"The first time I saw you, I wanted so badly to be near you. Even though I knew you were dangerous, I couldn't help myself." I am almost shy as I speak.

"Dangerous?" she asks.

I look away, studying the pristine wall. She could have done anything to me in ND3—beat me, raped me, given me to a male guard—of course I didn't know then she would never do such things to anyone.

"Yes, dangerous." I look up and she stares at me for a long time. Finally, I say, "I'm sorry, Rachel. I'm sorry for all the crappy circumstances that have brought us to where and who we are today."

"I'm sorry, too."

I want more than ever to take her into my arms, but know better. I distract myself instead.

"Shall I go get you some supplies, or are you able to go yourself?"

"I am able. You'll show me where to go?"

"Of course."

†

It is when we are leaving the large pantry that Heart turns to me.

"What is that vibration? Do you feel it, or am I just still having issues with the altitude?"

"No, there is indeed a vibration."

"A buzzing?"

"Yes, and a buzzing. It's the bees."

"The bees?"

"Would you like to see? Maybe before it's time to leave I can show you."

"Really? Is it safe?" Her eyes grow wide.

"Yes, it is safe."

We are only back at our quarters for a few minutes when there is a knock at the door. It is Carlos and Nell with the supplies I am to begin sorting and organizing for the upcoming trip. Our bedding is moved together to one side to make room for the supplies.

"Something big is about to happen?" Heart asks after they leave.

"Yes, a journey to join Gotham and Breanne."

She watches me as I sort. I glance in her direction a few times, hoping she will say what is on her mind.

"You would have been in grave danger had the guards at ND3 known you were General Brodie's daughter."

"Yes, I would have been."

"I am glad you were strong and never gave your name."

"I am as well," I say.

"Do you still wish me to have this?" she asks as she holds up the bracelet I'd made for her.

"Would you like me to tie it on for you?" I smile. I hold my breath waiting for her answer.

"I would like that."

I tie the hemp strings together on her left wrist without touching her skin. She holds it up to look closer at it.

"It is beautiful. Thank you."

"You are welcome," I whisper. I glance at how our bedding is together in one corner and feel nervous about trying to sleep with her that close to me.

Later, once in the bedding, I feign sleep when she cuddles up to my back. I do not know if she is already asleep when she does so, and I don't really want to know. I am happy letting myself believe it is intentional.

†

With Suzanna's blessing, I take Heart through the maze of tunnels until we get to the interior wall of the bee caves. This is a big deal. There is a long window through which to glimpse the bee activity, but other than that, it's just a dark wall that literally vibrates with the energy and activity of the bees on the other side.

I remember the first time Breanne brought me to feel the bees. I was mesmerized. I knew at the time that it took a lot for them to trust me, so young and silly I was, and I will forever be grateful to Breanne for showing me, and Suzanna for allowing her to do so.

I touch the wall below the window with both hands, palms flat against it. Heart mirrors my action and immediately smiles. The buzz is incessant and loud and if not for knowing the beauty of it, could be terrifying to hear and feel.

Heart's excitement is palpable. I catch myself about to touch her arm, or hand, to guide her attention in one direction or another with a soft touch to the face, but I know better. I will not risk getting the reaction of contempt by touching her, however innocent my motivation.

"That was amazing," she says, as we begin to wind back through the dimly lit maze of the tunnel.

I have to smile at her joy. I want to tell her that she is amazing, but I keep that to myself.

"Why are there bees?"

"Would you rather bats?" I tease.

"There are bats, too?" Her eyes grow wide.

"No, there are no bats here. These bees are a hybrid of those that were in this country before the poison killed so many of them, and another, heartier type that the founders of Karst carefully cultivated to flourish in the caves. They are how the farms in this area can grow such a variety of crops."

She watches me with interest in my words and I hate to end this time with her.

"Would you like to see the gardens?" I ask.

"On the outside?" Her eyes widen.

"Follow me." I laugh. I lead her away from the main corridor until the lamps are no longer supplying most of the light, and the opening to the outside is in view. I climb the steps carved into the wall and beckon for her to follow me.

"An entrance," she whispers. Just then Andre sticks his head in the opening from the outside and she is startled. "Oh."

"Hi, Andre," I say.

"Hello, Kai." He smiles. He turns and nods at Heart. "Hello, Rachel."

"Hi. I want to let her peek out at the gardens. We aren't actually going down to them."

He steps away, leaving the opening clear. I nod for Heart to come up behind me, and I stay vigilant. I want to make sure she doesn't falter, but I won't touch her unless it is absolutely necessary.

"Oh, my," she says when she looks out. "The garden has rows and rows!"

"It isn't visible from the other side of the mountain." I gesture to the north of the garden, where the charred earth is black and barren. "And no one comes from the scorched lands."

I indicate the path that winds down, and the pulley system used to bring up the produce.

"Some of the farmers live in those homes on the side there," I say as I point. "Some of the people of Karst work the gardens as well."

"This is amazing," she whispers.

Andre and I exchange smiles.

"Maybe one day you'll go down and see it up close," he says.

Heart looks at me and I shrug.

"Maybe so." I hate to go now, to break away from such a moment, but I must meet with the others.

When we make it back to the stark white of the main corridor, Heart almost looks disappointed that I am taking my leave.

Within the hour of my leaving Heart at the door to our quarters, I am with the council, sitting around the low table. Even as I sit here, still in close proximity to where Heart is, I miss her presence. I must broach the subject now.

"I will leave it up to Rachel as to whether or not she wants to accompany us."

"Wait—you will what?" Shelton asks.

"I will let Rachel decide."

"Why would you even think for a second that it's okay for her to go?"

"I am responsible for her." I cross my arms over my chest.

"I don't know what this thing is between you two, but there just might be a time you will have to choose between the movement and her." Shelton leans closer to me.

"If the *movement* is forcing the choice, I will choose her." I glare at him. "There is to be no doubt about that."

"Maybe you should stay here with her," Shelton says.

"Maybe we will let Gotham and Breanne decide my role when we meet up with them," I snap back.

"Enough," Dawson says.

The meeting breaks up after we discuss the logistics and supply situation, and I return to quarters.

I want to take care in how I approach Rachel about whether she wants to stay or come with me. I don't want to influence her decision. I am not even sure myself which will be harder, to have her with me, the constant reminder of what I cannot have, or have her stay here, in which case I will not know definitively at any given time if she is safe and happy.

"Do you like it here?" I ask her.

"Yes. Very much. Thank you for bringing me here with you."

"Would you like to stay? You know, make this your home?"

"You believe there is something productive I could do here? I know you will always have a place here, but are you sure they will continue to welcome me permanently?"

"You will continue to have a place here." I hesitate. "They will find something productive for you to do."

"And you? What will you do here?" she asks.

I can feel her eyes on me, even with my gaze averted. Finally, I look at her.

Heart watches me for a few moments.

"You do not plan to stay, do you?"

"I have a job to do, and that job is elsewhere." I nervously bite my lower lip. "My job is to find Gotham and Breanne, and to help them with the Peace Movement."

"I see." Heart's shoulders droop and she blinks fast, as if fighting tears. "You do not want me with you."

"I thought you liked Karst." My heart wants to drag her with me everywhere I go, but my head is telling me to discourage her. I am at odds with myself.

"I do like it here. I love the people of Karst. I want to be here, but I want to be here with you."

"I cannot in good faith stay when there is so much to do for the movement, for the future."

"Then please let me go with you."

"It is rough and dirty and dangerous out there." I know my words are not convincing, and if I am to be honest with myself, I do not care for them to be.

"You don't want me to go with you," she says.

"That is not true."

"You don't want to be with me."

"Of course I do. I do want to be with you, but more than that, I want you to be safe. Here, you will be safe." I take a deep breath.

"Please, let me accompany you," she pleads.

"As you wish. But only come with me if you can be in full support of the Peace Movement." I am not strong enough to try harder to convince her to stay.

"You have my full support, as does the Peace Movement. I will go with you."

"If you stay—"

"I said I will go with you," she responds.

"Then it's settled." I am relieved and scared at the same time. When I look up again, she is pressing her lips against the bracelet I made for her, looking a million miles away.

We sit quietly for a long time.

"Why do you look so sad?" she asks, breaking the silence.

I do not know how to respond to her, so I say nothing.

"Kai, please."

"The way you affect me…" I glance up for a moment, then look way again. "Sometimes I think it was so much easier back in ND3."

"Why would you say something like that?"

She must think I've lost my mind. I try to explain.

"I didn't feel guilty when I looked at you then. I only felt yearning, even if it was painful at times. Now I feel yearning *and* guilt. It's just too much sometimes."

"Do not feel guilty. I made the choice to come with you."

"But you didn't know the whole story. I held back my suspicions of the details because I wanted you with me so badly." I look up and hold her gaze.

"But you do not any longer."

"Don't say that," I say. "Why would you say that?"

"Because you haven't kissed me once since we've been free."

I want to remind her that she has recoiled from my touch even when it was done innocently, therefore there was no way I would reach for her intimately. I do not state the obvious.

"That would be wrong."

"How was it okay then and not now?" she asks.

"Because the power dynamics have shifted."

She stares at me.

I am pretty sure that she has known all along that I wait for her to instigate intimate, physical contact. Is she subconsciously punishing me for having all the power now? But did I? If Heart can render me without breath and words, then didn't she hold all the power still?

"Kai," she whispers.

I lean closer to better hear her.

"Come here."

I go closer still and her lips find the corner of my mouth. She caresses the side of my face and puts enough pressure in her touch to bring my mouth fully onto hers. I feel the contact with every cell in my body.

At first I am very still when her tongue slips into my mouth. I am afraid to move and maybe break the spell, but soon I cannot resist exploring her mouth with my tongue as well. I have never felt anything like this joining of our mouths before.

I start to cry out when she moves away, ending the kiss, but then her mouth trails along the line of my jaw, over to my earlobe, down my neck. A tiny groan escapes me.

"Is this okay?" she asks, her voice a whisper.

"Yes, yes, this is perfect."

Her tongue traces my collarbone and I gasp.

"I want to make love to you."

"Yes," I answer. "Just—just know this is my first time being intimate. I don't want to do anything wrong."

"You will do everything right, trust me." Her lips find mine.

"But—what if I don't *know* what to do?"

"Hold tightly to me, love. I will lead the way." She pulls my shirt over my head. I reach to do the same to hers and cannot believe how beautiful her breasts are.

I believe what she says. And I trust her. And when her hands find my breasts, I know we can do anything. Her thumbs draw circles around my nipples, and then she splays her hands over my breasts. My nipples pucker.

"I love how our skin contrasts," she whispers. "You are the most beautiful color I've ever seen."

I look at her pale hand on my darker flesh and smile. "Our skin tones do look perfect together."

My nipples harden further with her touch and I reach for her breasts and marvel at their softness. She kneels over me and slips my pants off but removes my hand from her pants when I reach to do the same. I think to complain but that thought is lost when her fingers find the wetness that has pooled between my legs.

"Oh," I say, surprised at the intensity of her touch.

"Okay?"

"Perfect." I slip my hand down the front of her cotton pants and am overwhelmed with joy when I find her wetness. My body arcs up to meet her touch. "You feel perfect, Rachel."

Her name feels so sweet on my lips that I say it again. "Rachel…"

We rock against each other's fingers while our mouths crash together in a searing kiss. I wonder for a moment about her past experience, who has touched her before me, but I don't want to know right now, that is a question for another day. I cry out as my body jerks and spasms, all control lost. Then she is mirroring my movement and we ride a wave of passion and release that leaves me simultaneously spent and energized.

I am overwhelmed and cannot stop the tears.

"I didn't hurt you, did I?" she asks.

"No, I am—overjoyed." I embrace her harder. A thought comes unbidden to me. *I would die for this woman. And I would kill for this woman.*

I roll us over so that I am on top. I pepper her face and neck with light kisses, lingering at her chin just long enough to run my tongue over the slight ridge of the scar, right where the bone ends and soft flesh begins.

"I want to feel your skin against mine," I say as I tug at the waistband of her pants. "Please."

She stares at me for several moments before she gives a slight nod.

I slip her pants down, slowly, watching her face for signs of increasing discomfort. She holds my gaze and I continue.

When she is naked below me, I lower my weight onto her and nuzzle my face into her neck. She smells delicious. I kiss her collarbone and then trail my lips over first one nipple, then the other. Gooseflesh rises on her skin.

"I want to know every inch of you," I whisper. "Every beautiful inch."

I trace my fingertips along her side, then let my touch drift to her hip. When I move to caress her buttock, she flinches. I feel the distinct ridge of a scar, then another and another.

I still my hand. "Roll over? Please."

She closes her eyes before doing as I ask.

"What is this?" Cross-shaped scars are spread across her buttocks and the back of her thighs.

"It is my penance for being a half-breed." She looks over her shoulder at me with an expression I cannot read.

"What?"

"Prayer Day was also penance day for me." I see shame on her face before she looks away.

"Penance? I don't understand. How are you a half-breed?"

"My mother was Anointed."

"Yes. Your father wasn't?"

"No."

I stare at her. I don't understand what she is saying.

"My father was a Resister. A guard at ND3." She looks away again.

I am beginning to get a disturbing picture. I swallow past the lump growing in my throat.

"He raped my mother. The head of ND3 was kind enough to let my mother keep me. Not all women got to keep their offspring."

"What happened to your mother?" My heart pounds and I ask, even though I'm afraid of the answer.

"She was killed in the Christian Revolution, when the Anointed took over power from the Resisters."

I stare at her. My head is aching and my stomach is roiling with acid.

"I was five years old. The new regime let me stay, when I was old enough they gave me a job, but they never let me forget that I was not truly one of theirs."

"I'm sorry," I whisper. I give one scar a ginger touch. I reach up and gently caress the lone scar under her chin.

"That one happened when I was a baby. An accident, I'm told."

I give a slight nod and again touch one of the scars on her buttock.

"I'm sorry," I repeat.

She rolls out from under me and nods her head. "It is all in the past now."

"Yes, it is. You are one of the tribe here at Karst. You are accepted wholeheartedly here, and here." I place my hand over my heart at the end of the statement. She covers mine with her own.

I bring her hand to my lips and kiss each finger softly. I want to continue my journey to know her entire body with my mouth.

"May I please kiss you? Everywhere?"

"Yes, Kai, yes."

I kiss every part of my sweet Rachel until she begs me to stop.

†

It is decided that everyone going on the expedition will get a fabricated UV tattoo on their shoulder. Mine and Rachel's tattoos are altered just enough that they won't scan properly. The fake and altered tattoos will glow under the black light scanners but should not be readable.

After, Suzanna approaches Rachel and me.

"Wouldn't you like Janna to polish up your haircuts?"

"You don't like the rough look?" I pretend to be appalled.

"Your hair could use some shaping up now that it is growing in," Suzanna says.

I smile at her, then turn to Rachel. "Would you like to be *polished*?"

"Only if you will as well."

"I suppose it is for the best." I ruffle my fingers through her hair.

Janna gives Rachel a layered look that truly flatters her face. My heart is pounding with desire, again, as I look at her.

When it is my turn, I close my eyes for a few moments before I will let Janna begin. I see the warrior within me and want to let her out full force.

Janna steps in front of me with the scissors.

"You will need the razor as well," I say with a smile.

Once again I am shorn, but only on the sides and back of my head. Janna leaves the top longer, where the thick, dark hair curls slightly.

When we go to the shower room to rinse off the hair, I want to join Rachel in her stall so badly that it hurts. I have too much respect for anyone who might come in, and so I keep my hands and eyes to myself while in there.

Back in our quarters, Rachel touches the hair that is barely there on the side of my head. She leans forward and kisses the mostly-revealed flesh there, then runs her fingers through the longer hair on the top of my head.

"You look like a warrior." She stares at me, a hand now on each side of my face.

"Is that pleasing to you?" I ask, hoping for an affirmative answer.

She kisses my top lip, my bottom lip, my right eyelid, my left.

"Everything about you pleases me," she whispers, her voice raspy. "I want to make love to you."

"You do, do you?" I grab her around the waist and pull her against me.

She presses harder against me. "Yes." She slips her hands under my shirt and cups my small breasts. Her thumbs rub against my nipples and I groan.

"You like that," she says, knowing the truth already.

I feel the warm wetness growing between my legs and know nothing but her mouth will help ease the desire threatening to overcome me. "Your mouth… please put your mouth on me."

"I can't wait to taste you." She smiles against my lips.

Her words excite me beyond what I've thought possible. My legs start to buckle and she eases me down onto the bedding, then lowers herself flush against me. She rocks against me for a few moments, then slides lower until her mouth finds its mark.

"Oh, Goddess," I whimper.

"Yes?"

"Yes, Rachel," I beg.

Her tongue strokes the length of my slick wetness. When she presses a finger against my opening, I take her hand in mine.

"Just your mouth," I say, hoping this is okay.

Her tongue and lips work me into a delicious release. She holds me until I stop shaking. I want to make her feel the same way and work my way down her body. When I kiss her wetness she reaches down between her legs and spreads herself open for me. The act renews my wetness and my breath catches in awe.

"Go inside me," she says.

I bring my hand between her legs and love how my fingers slip and slide there. I hesitate at her opening with a finger and she guides me inside her with her hand. She whimpers as I caress her from the inside before pulling out and pushing back in.

Her groans are driving me mad and I increase the speed with which I pump now two fingers in and out of her. My tongue continues to lash at her wetness and when her release comes it is hard, and the moans are loud, and it is the most amazing moment of my life.

PART FOUR—THE MISSION

CHAPTER NINE

There is much activity as we prepare to leave on our journey. Dawson is running around trying to help everyone with their supplies. I said my goodbyes to Heidi last night. The next time I see her she will be a mother. I tell myself this over and over, a promise to myself that I—we—will survive and return some day.

Emily approaches, says nothing, just gives me a quick hug, then hugs Rachel as well. She leaves just as quickly as she approached.

Suzanna calls me and Rachel over to her. She places a hand on the side of each of our faces and whispers a prayer to the Goddess. She smears rosemary oil across my forehead, then hesitates before touching Rachel.

Rachel nods her approval.

Suzanna smears the fragrant oil on Rachel's forehead.

"O Goddess of the galaxy, protect my daughters from harm."

She embraces me, then Rachel. When she pulls away there are tears in her eyes. I have never known her to cry before.

"We'll see you soon," I say, trying to sound braver than I feel.

"Stay safe, and above all, love one another," Suzanna says.

A small sob escapes Rachel and the sound shoots right through me. I watch her as Suzanna leaves us.

"You can change your mind," I remind her.

"No," she says, quickly. "There is no changing my mind. I will go with you to the ends of the earth if that is where you are going."

I kiss her on the lips, a soft lover's promise.

Jackson comes over, teasing. "Keep it decent."

He gives me a bow and arrow, then a pistol to strap to my calf. The gun feels awkward at first, but I am glad to have it just in case. Rachel turns down a bow, citing her inexperience as the reason, but does strap a sheath housing a large blade around her waist.

We leave Karst at first light. Our mission is to find Gotham and Breanne, then offer them whatever assistance they may need. Shelton, Jackson, Patricia, Carlos, and Nell have joined me and Rachel. It's a good-sized group, small enough to be agile, large enough to protect one another. We have horses, weapons, and a lot of hope.

Jackson and Patricia are together on a large stallion. Carlos and Nell each ride a mare. Shelton rides solo on a creamy, buckskin horse, his dark hands resting on its neck in stark contrast to the animal's light hair. I am on Shakespeare, a sturdy black gelding, with Rachel. The idea is that if we see any Resistance soldiers, Patricia will climb onto our horse after we jump off, and I will hide with Rachel. It will look then like only five people travel with the five horses. That is the plan, anyway. We are aware that it will be impossible to hide well once we hit the prairies, but while in the hill country we should be fine.

"Are you okay?" We are riding into the mountains, higher than we were at Karst or anywhere else, when I look over my shoulder.

"I am fine," Rachel says, holding tight to my hips.

This is her first time on a horse. When I learn this, I tell her to just hold on tight and follow my lead. This was the same advice she gave me when we made love for the first time. I feel a blush creep up my neck. I narrate what I am doing with my legs or the reins and describe the horse's gait when we trot or cantor, so she can learn.

Her head presses against the middle of my back.

"Does your head still ache?" I ask.

"A little."

"Drink some more water," I urge her.

Rachel is having some altitude issues again. She must stay hydrated if the headache is to abate. I can make it on very little provisions, so I give her much of my water ration.

Our group takes it slow. The horses must be reined in often as it is treacherous to travel along the crevasses left behind from the pre-war fracking, through the war's bombed-out wasteland, and the drought and fire-scarred land. I am relieved that we won't be traveling on land as ruined and scorched as the North territories.

It is not lost on us that getting to Gotham and Breanne may be the hardest part of the mission. Once we join with the others we will have safety in numbers, and we will know exactly what is required of us. Not knowing is hard.

Our strategy is to eat light while riding. We don't plan to stop during the day except to nourish and rest the horses. Rachel hands me strips of dried fruit from the pack tied behind her. I glance over my shoulder often, wanting to see her, wanting to make sure she's drinking and eating enough.

Shakespeare becomes a little edgy when a coywolf gets quite close to our group, the horse's muscles twitching against my lower legs, but then he relaxes a little. I take stock of the coywolf, and it's one of the darkest, thinnest canines I've ever seen, all legs and ears. Rachel holds on tighter to me.

"Do not worry," I say. I tell her things about other animals we might come upon: boar, rabbits, raccoons, possums, bats. "There is a book at Karst—when we return there I will show you pictures of so many animals that were once found in this land."

"Where did they go?" Rachel asks.

"Some became extinct because of loss of habitat or starvation. Some died because of the great rabies—a sickness some speculate might have been man-made." I turn to look at her as I speak. She is wide-eyed. Her innocence seems unending.

We are rounding a group of boulders when Shelton whistles. Jackson answers with a coywolf yip that is so realistic, I look over at the animal that is still following us, before realizing it is Jackson's signal for approaching soldiers or strangers.

Rachel and I climb down off Shakespeare and duck behind the boulders as Patricia climbs up into the saddle in our place. The dark coywolf is crouched behind a leafless bush, between us and what I believe to be two soldiers. Rachel is squeezing my hand so tight that my fingers are losing their sensation.

As we crouch behind the boulder, I keep one hand in Rachel's and the other resting against the holstered firearm still strapped to my leg. I have no doubt that I will kill to protect this woman, my lover.

The soldiers ride up to our party and they halt. There are indeed only the two of them. I can barely make out a word here and there, but know what they are doing when Carlos pulls his shirt off his shoulder. The taller of the two soldiers waves the scanner over the UV ink, pulls it away, taps it against the palm of his hand and tries again. Then he tries to scan Nell's tattoo.

"Is that thing even on?" Shelton asks, perhaps a little too loudly.

The guard tries to scan Shelton as well.

My attention is drawn away from them when I hear a low growl. The coywolf looks as if about to pounce and I am confused over what is happening. Then the animal springs out from behind the bush and rushes at the shorter guard's horse. The tall guard draws his gun but can't get a shot amidst all of the horses' legs.

Shakespeare rears up and chaos ensues.

"Shoot that beast!" a soldier yells as he points at the coywolf.

"I don't have a shot without hitting a horse."

The coywolf runs to the other side of our group and Shelton's horse rears up on his hind legs.

Carlos says something I can't make out and one of the soldiers yells, "Resist!" before both ride off.

The others give an unenthusiastic "Resist" back, to appease the retreating soldiers.

The coywolf has circled back now, and is only twenty or thirty feet from us. He is panting.

"He's thirsty," Rachel says.

"It appears so," I say as I watch Patricia and Jackson come closer. I walk over to Patricia who is still astride Shakespeare.

"Let me get my cup," I say.

She looks at me as if I am insane as I pour water into the cup, set it down between me and the animal, then back away. He hesitates, then moves in to drink the water.

"What the heck?" Nell says.

"Look at that. He's very thirsty." Rachel has come up behind me and takes my hand.

"We shouldn't be encouraging the animal," Shelton complains.

"The animal just saved all of our asses," Jackson says.

I watch as the coywolf cuts its eyes in my direction while lapping up the water. In a flash, recognition settles over me, and when our eyes lock, I know I am already acquainted with this creature's soul.

"We should get moving." Carlos rides closer.

Nell looks up and I follow her gaze. Two vultures soar in a lazy circle above us, their black heads and wings in stark contrast to the light-blue sky.

The coywolf scoots farther away and I pick up my empty cup. Carlos raises his eyebrows at me and I mumble, "I will clean it when we next stop." Within minutes Rachel and I are back on Shakespeare and our group is on its way again, coywolf included.

†

The horses are grazing on what little plants are on the prairie. Carlos, Patricia, and Shelton are hunting, while Jackson and Nell tend to our gear. Rachel and I are harvesting kudzu leaves for a salad, and the roots to both boil for dinner and to dry for tea later. We are filling sacks with leaves and roots when we stumble upon a patch of drought-resistant blackberries. We pick some of the berries, happy to be able to surprise the others with the tasty fruit when we all gather back for our meal.

I feed a juicy blackberry to Rachel. The look on her face warms me. She feeds me one as well, and when she lets the tip of her finger enter my mouth, and leaves it there for a breathy moment, I feel the heat and wetness grow between my legs. I remember we are out of sight of the others and smile. When she turns away from me to begin harvesting again, I grab her around the waist and pull her to me, her back to my front. I nuzzle into her neck.

"I've wanted to touch you like this for days."

She turns her head enough to capture my lips with hers. Heat sears through me. She twists around to face me and our breasts press together through the material of our shirts.

"Touch me now," she whispers. "Like this." She pushes against me and rocks her hips, the heat of our friction making me wetter.

We rub our bodies against one another, through our clothing, causing a fast and hard release that leaves us gasping against each other. I want to taste her so badly it hurts, but I appreciate this stolen moment nonetheless.

At our meal, the others are happy for blackberries to go with their kudzu. We eat quickly. As the horses are already watered and rested, it's time for us to resume our journey. I feel sensitive where my body touches the saddle, and the memory of our intimacy makes me smile.

We've been riding a couple of hours when we pause on a ridge. To the north large dark clouds give way to the vertical gray striations below them that are indicative of heavy rain.

"The downpours are starting in the north," Shelton says.

"It will be weeks, if not months, before they make it to us." I add, "Other than the slight drizzle that will tease us before that."

Shelton nods his agreement.

"What's that?" Rachel asks, as she points below us to the south, in the valley.

Clusters of round and rectangular holding areas for water, and the adjacent Employment Center, sprawl out below us.

"That's a water processing plant. On the west side of it is an internment camp—aka Employment Center."

"And that field?"

"Hemp."

"Where are the retirement centers?" Rachel asks.

"What?" I ask.

"The retirement centers. I've seen detention and employment centers, but no retirement ones."

My stomach lurches. Could this sweet, sweet woman be so naïve that she thinks prisoners actually retire?

"She's serious?" Shelton asks.

"Don't say it." I level a glare at him.

I will have a talk with Rachel later when we bed down. I want it to come from me that the old and infirm inmates she must have thought were going to retirement centers were really being taken somewhere for—well, disposal.

I hear Rachel's quick intake of breath as she leans closer to me.

"I am a fool. There are no retirement centers?" She squeezes my hips tighter. "Tell me."

"No, there are no retirement centers. There never have been. I am sorry." I turn my upper body to look at her but she has pressed her face into me and I cannot see her expression.

†

We travel west for quite some time, then start going north. It is a long few weeks before we find my siblings. When we do, Gotham and Breanne are surrounded by hostiles, struggling with their smaller group to not be overcome.

"Ferals," Shelton calls out.

We can see the battle scene in its entirety from our position. I would know the twins' silhouettes anywhere. Breanne's dark, shoulder length hair is pulled back away from her face but Gotham's, also long, swings free.

I watch as several fighters lunge at each other, still on horseback, with swords and knives. Some are on the ground, fighting with fists and such great fury that I believe they will fight to the death.

My party rides our horses hard, straight at the center of the group that battles my siblings, causing the Ferals to disperse.

In the confusion that follows, I see a Feral rider knock Gotham from his horse. I steer Shakespeare toward my brother. Gotham's loose hair falls into his face and I cannot see his eyes to know in what direction he looks. A large man approaches Gotham from what I assume is his blind spot, a heavy club held over his head, but when my mouth opens I know my warning is lost in the surrounding noise.

158

I draw an arrow back on the bowstring, take a deep breath, and let it fly at the man about to bludgeon my beloved brother. Just before he swings downward at Gotham's head, my arrow rips into his chest. He stops mid-motion, drops the club, and then falls to his knees.

The man releases a death-scream before Gotham pushes him off balance and into the dirt, and it brings attention to my brother. Everyone looks around and I feel many gazes finding me behind the bow. The sight of me sitting upon Shakespeare, with the bow held in front of me and Rachel behind me, brings attention to us, unwanted attention, but at least it has stilled the Feral combatants for a moment.

I pull out another arrow and ready it to protect myself and Rachel.

Gotham jumps back onto his horse and lets out an ear-splitting war cry. The Ferals are overcome by the new numbers as our small group joins the twins' fighters. Those Ferals, who are left alive and capable, flee.

I ride up beside my brother.

"About damn time you got here, little sister," Gotham teases.

I don't look at him. My focus is glued on the man lying in the dirt at the feet of Gotham's horse. I have never killed anyone before. Am I a hypocrite to kill in the name of peace? I don't have time to think too much about it, as Breanne calls us over to her.

I quickly understand that Gotham and Breanne are major players in this quest for peace. They are not just a small cog in the machine, they *are* the machine. They have a small contingent with them now, but have plans to meet up with a larger group within days. There had just been the small inconvenience of this battle to live through first.

As we ride, I catch glimpses of several vultures overhead. When I look at the scrawny coywolf still following us, I'm convinced the scavenging birds think he's meant to be a meal for them soon. I will have to try to put some meat on his bones.

We ride north for a few hours, then set up camp. I can't help but smile every time I look at the twins as we sit around the small fire. I have missed them so.

"We have company," Breanne says.

I follow her gaze to our coywolf. "Yes, he's with us."

She quirks her eyebrow upward. "Do tell."

"That is Ajax." His name pops into my head, seemingly out of nowhere. "He helped us get out of a situation with some Resistance soldiers earlier."

A man named Shawn sits beside Breanne. "Hey, Bre. All the horses have been cared for."

I wonder about the tender glance that passes between them. As I understand it, he is one of the Franklinites who joined Breanne and Gotham early in the movement. He looks over toward the coywolf.

"That's Ajax." My sister gives him a dazzling smile.

He grins. When one of his men hand him a plate of roasted rabbit, he breaks off a piece and throws it over to the loitering coywolf.

Rachel sits down next to me and we share a plate of roasted vegetables and boiled kudzu root. When Shawn offers us some rabbit, I tell him no thanks. I look to Rachel, hoping she isn't shy about taking what she wants. She glances at me.

"Take some if you wish," I whisper.

She shyly takes a small piece and thanks Shawn.

I look around and study the diverse group of people who sit around the fire, quietly eating and conversing with one another. I am proud of my brother and sister for unifying these different groups together for peace. I am proud of myself for coming to their aid, and I am proud of everyone with us for fighting the good fight.

Later, we are about to bed down, when Gotham comes to me.

"Tell me about Rachel," he says.

"What do you want to know?"

"You are obviously coupled." He watches Rachel who is across the clearing as he addresses me.

"Yes."

Breanne joins us.

"Are you interrogating her about her companion?" Breanne asks.

"Yes, Bre, you are just in time. She's just now starting to blush," Gotham teases as he tucks his hair behind his ears. He ruffles the longer hair at the top of my head. "She's looking so grown up now that she's having sex."

"Stop." I bat his hand away from my hair.

Breanne laughs. "She's very pretty."

"And pale," Gotham adds.

"Yes, and pale," Breanne says with a smile. She studies me for several moments. "Do you love her?"

Breanne's question catches me off guard. The playful tone is no longer in her voice.

"Yes, I love her."

"Do you trust her?" Gotham nods.

"With my life," I say without hesitation. "And I will protect her—with my life."

"I see." Breanne stares at me. She looks hard and soft all at once and it makes me wonder how much I really know my sister.

I look at Breanne, then Gotham. I glance at Rachel and my heart pounds.

"I need something from you both." I have their attention. "I need you to promise me that no matter what happens, you will protect Rachel."

"Of course we will—we vow to do our best to protect everyone in the Peace Movement," Gotham says.

"But if something happens to me you will look out for her—care for her as if she is your own flesh and blood."

Breanne raises an eyebrow.

I know they do not understand completely, so I continue. "If it becomes my life or hers, you must promise me you'll keep her safe."

"You cannot mean for us to choose a stranger over our sister," Breanne says.

"I do. Please, I chose this life, Rachel did not. Not really."

"Look around you, Kai. Do you think anyone here truly *chose* this life?" Breanne asks.

"Please," I beg. "Please just promise me you will always take care of her."

"Okay," Gotham says. "We promise."

Now that I am seeing a side to Breanne that I've never seen before, I wonder how much control Gotham will have over decisions like that. Breanne is very much in control of everyone and everything. I find the dynamics interesting.

There is a flurry of activity on the outermost part of our camp. New riders join us. Gotham lets out a short whistle and everyone gathers around. We are close to fifty people now. Everyone looks at Breanne.

Gotham lets out another short whistle and everyone quiets.

Breanne steps up onto a boulder.

"The thing about peace is that sometimes it takes everything but peace to make it happen." She looks around at those surrounding her. "We need warriors who are willing to go against the values of peace in order for it to be attained. If you are not on board with this, then you need to stay behind tomorrow morning when we ride. We can meet back with you later, but tomorrow's fight for peace will not be peaceful."

I am nodding my head.

Breanne turns to face me. "What's it going to be Kai?"

"I am with you." The image of the man I shot earlier flashes through my mind.

"You will be going against our father," she adds.

"I am not my father's loyal little soldier." I hold her gaze. I think of the conversation I'd overheard, about me sacrificing Rachel for the Resistance, and stand taller. "I am a warrior for peace!"

Several people around us applaud.

"Rachel?" Breanne asks.

"I, too, am with you." She looks at Breanne as she speaks, but then turns to me. She looks so shy, yet strong, standing in front of me, stating her intent, that I wish I could embrace her. She was, and is, my own warrior, and I love her so.

"Shelton?"

"I am wholly on board."

"Jackson?"

"Peace at any price," he says loudly.

Breanne continues her rollcall, naming those whom she knows personally, nodding at those she does not, and all answer in the affirmative.

When I finally take my eyes off Rachel and look back to my sister, I see she is every bit the leader and warrior that we need to make this happen. I am so very proud of her.

We are to bed down early, for we leave at first light. I notice that Breanne is sharing bedding with Shawn. I push my bedding over until it touches Rachel's. She smiles and my soul sings.

†

The next morning, no one stays behind when we ride. Breanne sits so high and straight in her saddle that I know she must be proud of her people.

We skirt around ND2, the male equivalent of ND3, and note the absence of guards or soldiers outside. In the distance is a church, complete with a steeple. I know we are getting closer to the danger of being seen when we hear the church bells. I glance behind me at Rachel. Do I expect to see her cross herself, bow her head, or mumble a prayer? What I do see is an expression of uncertainty bordering on terror.

Beyond the church is the military settlement we are heading to, the one we will conquer.

When we break for the midday meal, Breanne and Gotham talk with a dozen people before calling everyone together. Breanne tells us we are stopping for the day, that the next morning we will attack our target.

"Rest this afternoon. Remember to keep hydrated. We ride over the ridge and into the settlement to overtake it first thing tomorrow morning."

I think to find a private place to spend intimate time with Rachel, but Shawn has offered to coach Rachel in archery. My initial thought is that I should have been teaching her all along, but I know that he will probably be a better instructor than I.

At first she is shy about learning, but in no time she is hitting the target and becoming proud of her progress. I am proud of her as well.

By the end of the afternoon, Rachel's practice with Shawn has paid off. If she keeps progressing at this rate, she will be an expert archer in no time. After practice is over, she comes to me as I prepare vegetables for roasting.

"Are we almost out of vegetables?"

"Yes, soon all that will be left are the pickled okra, and the kudzu we've been harvesting along the way."

It is obvious to me her mind isn't on our food supply. Finally, she says, "It's one thing to shoot an arrow at a target against a boulder, but another altogether to shoot at a person."

"Yes, killing someone is—heart breaking." I think about the man I shot in defense of my brother. "It's not something to be taken lightly."

"I would never take it lightly. But I would kill to protect my lover," she says as she grasps my arm. "And to protect my people."

"As would I." I look around at our ever-growing numbers and think *yes, our people*.

We gather around the fire for dinner and Breanne talks to us when we finish eating, telling us what is next.

The plan is to overtake the settlement on the other side of the ridge and then to join with a group in McNally before taking over an army settlement to its North. At both settlements, we will disarm the Resistance soldiers and take their supplies. How they are treated after that will depend greatly on them, we are told.

"Kai," Breanne says. "In the morning, you and Rachel are to take a group of ten to fifteen and go just east of the camp, cutting it off from McNally. You will be scouting for any stragglers from the settlement that the rest of us will ride against. Go as far as that first stand of trees, then turn back toward this camp."

I want to engage in argument as to why I should go with the fighting group, but Breanne's steely glare stops me.

"As you wish," I say.

The next morning, I ride with Rachel behind me, leading Jackson, Patricia, and twelve others to the east as instructed. We all have strung bows tethered to our backs. The gun I have yet to fire is still strapped to my leg.

Ajax stays with us, as I expected he would. I notice he is filling out—no longer all legs and ears—and wonder if he is doing so because of a steadier diet, or because he is just now growing into adulthood. He's still darker than any coywolf I've ever seen, and his eyes hold so much expression that I expect at any minute to be able to read his thoughts. I glance up and right away notice the absence of vultures. This pleases me.

We ride east, then sweep back toward the camp as instructed. All we see are clouds building to the north. There are no soldiers escaping the settlement and no one else comes from other areas to take on our warriors. The day is not exciting, but we have completed our mission successfully when Breanne and the others rejoin us in camp. They are loaded down with confiscated supplies, and lead a small group of prisoners.

"They fought as if their hearts weren't quite in it, to be honest." Breanne sits beside me at the fire before dinner.

"Perhaps we can overcome the Resistance with words instead of force?" I ask.

"One day, maybe. But for right now, we cannot expect anything good from the Resistance soldiers." She nods her head in the direction of the prisoners being guarded on the other side of the camp. "We will carefully vet these people to see if they are Peace Warriors in the making."

"And if they aren't considered redeemable?" I study them from a safe distance and imagine they could easily be the same soldiers who freed me from ND3. They could also be the same soldiers who might have hurt or killed Rachel.

"They will go to a prison set up in McNally. We will give them the benefit of the doubt, even though most likely, they would not have given that to the Anointed." Breanne looks at Rachel as she says this.

Rachel looks away, stares into the fire.

†

The next morning, we head toward McNally. I am still the best scout in our ranks, so I am tasked to go round a thick stand of trees on foot to determine if the last settlement between us and our destination can be taken from the enemy. I go on foot.

I am just upon the tree line, still barely within sight of the others, when I hear a low growl. I look behind me and see

Ajax facing to my left. I see a movement and know he was warning me of the presence of someone else.

I slip behind a large tree and take a deep breath. Now the growling is louder and the movement is coming from many directions. Light catches off the barrel of a gun. I place my hand on my own gun and pull it out. Before I can level it at any a target, the movement is so thick and so fast that I know I am surrounded. I shove the gun, then the holster, under the root of the tree I am behind and start to walk slowly back in the direction I came from.

"Show your hands!" the shouts come from all around me. I drop to my knees and put my hands up. Anger bubbles up inside me—at them for obvious reasons and at myself for not being able to evade them.

From my lower vantage point I can see through the trees and catch a glimpse beyond the tree line of Gotham holding Rachel back, his hand over her mouth to quiet her as she struggles to break free. He is keeping his promise to me and I love him more than ever at that moment.

Ajax is running frantically back and forth. A soldier is sighting his weapon while staring at the coywolf. I concentrate, trying to will him to go back to the safety of the others but he doesn't respond until a series of yips come from where the others are hiding. Ajax shifts directions and runs toward them, causing the soldier's bullet to miss him.

Every Resistance soldier in my sight has a firearm and I am glad that Breanne didn't try to lead our warriors against them, even if it means the worse for me.

My hands are bound in front of me and I'm forced to walk alongside the soldiers' horses as I'm led toward the intact portion of the North-South Highway. Three of the men walk behind me and every time one of them believes me to be walking too slowly, I am given a shove. We follow the highway that I have stayed mostly away from—the soldiers have no reason to skirt the road as they are not trying to outmaneuver anyone, so we make good time.

Raymond, a young man I have known my entire life, levels a hard glare at me.

"Stop dragging along!"

I take a deep breath to settle myself and don't answer.

A soldier I don't recognize pushes me so hard from behind that I stumble. I take several foot-tangled steps before I lose my balance and hit the cracking pavement of the hard road. I've landed on my knees, which hurts, but I am thankful not to have landed on my previously injured shoulder. I am yanked up off the ground by the collar of my shirt.

"Raymond," the soldier who has grabbed me hollers. "We are losing time. Put her on a horse. Hog tie her and lay her on the horse's ass if you have to."

Raymond stares at me with a look between embarrassment and contempt.

"If you give me a hand up I will sit in front of you and not cause you any trouble," I say in a low voice.

He's fiddling with a length of rope. When he approaches me with it, while glancing at my feet, I say, "Come on, Raymond."

He kneels in front of me and starts to tie my feet. I kick at him, not hard, just trying to get him to drop the nonsense about binding me further. In just seconds, another soldier throws me to the ground while a third one straddles me.

"This isn't necessary," I mutter.

"Oh, isn't it?" someone asks.

My hands are untied, brought behind my back, and roughly retied tighter. My feet are bound together. I try to buck away as someone lifts me and lays me over the front of the horse's saddle like a bag of garbage.

Every impact of the horse's hooves to the ground jolts my body in its unnatural position. I try to control my breathing, try to relax to move with the horse's steps instead of against them, but I am so angry that rage courses harshly through me, making me rigid and causing me pain.

We ride the entire day, and when we finally enter my family's homestead, we do so through the heavily guarded north entrance.

I'm dragged off the horse and deposited onto the ground while they untie my feet. Raymond assists another soldier in bringing me into the meeting room. I am thrown at my father's feet. He looms over me, his dark eyes empty.

"You treat my daughter like an animal?" he asks Raymond.

"She has fought us the entire way, sir."

"Of course she has." Father crosses his arms over his chest. "Remove the bindings."

The second man, the one I do not know, does as he is told and unties my hands.

"Leave us," Father says. Once we are alone, he gestures toward the chair to his left. I sit, and then he sits across the table from me.

"Let's talk, then I will see that you are given some food and water."

Weary of him, I just nod.

"Where are your siblings?"

"I do not know where they are." I look him in the eyes.

"Where is your Anointed concubine?"

I recoil at his words.

"I do not know her whereabouts either. I am traveling alone."

"Thirsty?" He pushes his mug in my direction. He smiles at me. "Take some shine, it'll make you feel better."

"No, thank you."

"Tell me about Rachel Prince," he says.

I try to hide my surprise but am pretty sure I fail miserably.

"Yes, daughter, I have seen the registration data."

I shrug, try to look disinterested.

"There is a guard with the last name Hart who is unaccounted for. Her family is concerned for her safety."

"That has nothing to do with me," I say, red flags rising higher and higher. I think of the story Rachel told me about the guard impregnating her mother and I don't trust a word my father spews at me.

"Oh, no?" he asks.

I breathe deeply and exhale loudly.

"I really don't know what you think I know. I don't know anyone named Hart. I was traveling with a Rachel Prince, a woman I knew who was incarcerated at ND3. I only registered her to me because she was undocumented and we just wanted to hurry through the reintroduction process."

"Where is Rachel Prince now?"

"I don't know. We have gone our separate ways. I, well, I lost interest in her, if you know what I mean." Bile surges into my throat with the story I fabricate.

"All we need to do is one blood test on your property. If she is not who we think she is, as you insist, that will be the end of that."

"And who is it exactly that you think she is?" I struggle to not show any emotion.

He does not answer me.

"One blood test, then she will be free to leave? If I were able to find her again to begin with, that is."

"Sure. You tell us where the girl is and we'll get our answers. Then you can leave with her." He scowls.

I stare at him. I know with every cell in my body that this is a trick, that he has no intention of freeing either of us once he gets his hands on her. I just wish I knew why she was so important to them.

"So, this Hart woman…why do you wish to locate her?"

"I am not here to answer your questions, girl. You are here to answer mine. And I would greatly appreciate it if you would begin to do so."

I nod my head and force my posture to look more relaxed.

"I am traveling alone, Father. I am in search of bee caves to begin bartering with the many groups of Independents throughout the country. I don't know where Gotham and Breanne are, and I have no idea where Rachel Prince is."

"Liar!" he shouts at me.

I say nothing.

"Jonas!"

Jonas enters the room.

"Take her to the cell. If she wants to protect that Anointed animal then she shall be treated like one as well." He turns his back on me.

Jonas grabs me by the arm and jerks me to my feet. The pain in my shoulder is sudden and brings back many bad memories of my incarceration at ND3. I am dragged to a jail that I didn't even know existed in the homestead, then bound by my hands over my head, secured by rope to a metal ring screwed into the ceiling.

After a few hours of standing there with my hands tied above my head, my father comes in, alone. He wants me to tell him the plan, to tell him what the twins are up to, to tell him where Rachel is.

I tell him nothing.

"I will happily take a trade—you for the Anointed girl."

I do not dignify it with a response.

"All I'd have to do is get word to Gotham and Breanne."

"Go right ahead," I say.

"You don't think they will give her up for you?"

"Over my dead body," I spit out, unable to control myself.

"Don't tempt me," he says, his voice icy.

He takes his leave, and soon after my nephew, Sebastian, comes into the cell. When I don't give in to his pleas for me to just tell them what they want to know, he screams at me that I am a traitor, then spits on me before storming out. I see that he has become much like his father, Lewis. I wonder if Lewis will be gracing me with his presence next.

The pain in my shoulder increases with each passing hour. My mouth is dry and I am feeling weak. My bladder screams to be emptied.

Father returns. He paces in front of me. It reminds me of when I was a child and he would ask me questions about my time out with Gotham and Breanne. He couldn't come right out and admit that, even then, he didn't trust the twins, so he would ask me questions of their business, the honey and produce they brought back as payment for protection of the small pockets of people living off the Anointed army's radar.

I didn't break under his pressure then, and I will not now.

"How much pain did the Anointed bring you in ND3?" He runs his finger across the scar above my eye.

It is not lost on me that the most physical pain inflicted on me while incarcerated did not actually come from the Anointed.

"What did they do to you in that prison?" He looks me over closely. "Who are you? You are not the level-headed, loyal soldier you were raised to be."

Raised? Doesn't he mean 'trained'? I think about how a daughter is raised and a soldier is trained, but do not differentiate that for him.

"If we do not take care of the Anointed now, and the power dynamic changes again, you will be the first to be rounded up and slaughtered." He glares at me. "You have soiled one of theirs—even if her pedigree isn't quite intact— and they will not forgive you that."

"Perhaps that is true, but I will not sit back and watch the atrocious behavior of genocide, not from those who claim to be my own people, or anyone else."

"Are Gotham and Breanne doing business with the Anointed?" he asks now.

The change in subject catches me off guard. Still, I do not respond.

"Are they planning a coup?"

I say nothing.

"You do understand that I must be tougher on you than any of the others here, right? You will be made an example. Your crime of treason is a capital offence. The people will not follow a leader who cannot even control his own offspring."

"And you think you will earn their admiration if you kill your own daughter?"

He's contemplative, but does not respond. He leaves me without another word.

My wrists ache. I can't quite wrap my head around the way things have turned out—to have survived the tyranny of the Anointed in ND3 just to die at the hands of my father's army is an assault to everything I've ever held dear. For once I am glad that my mother is dead so she doesn't have to give witness to these events. A lump grows in my throat and I wonder if I am meant to choke on my own sadness.

When Jonas enters, the look on his face clues me into the fact that I am in for a rough time of it.

"Ready to talk?" he asks.

I focus on his thick, bushy eyebrows and do not respond. He smacks me hard in the face. I still do not respond.

He punches me in the stomach and asks again, "Ready to talk?"

I am fighting to breathe against the pain when he kicks my legs out from under me. I dangle from my bound hands for several moments before getting steady on my feet again. He asks me if I'm ready to talk, I say nothing, he strikes me again.

This goes on for what feels like hours, but I assume is just minutes, before he starts to laugh.

"This is a dream come true for me. You've always been a smug little bitch, and now I can do whatever I want to you in the name of serving the General." He grabs my face and his fingers dig into me as he leers.

He jumps slightly at the sound of a knock at the door. A voice from outside informs Jonas that the General is requesting that he join him. He grabs me by the longer hair on the top of my head and twists until my face is angled to look up at him.

"Don't go anywhere," he says with a smile, and then he is gone.

Camryn barely makes a sound as she comes into the cell. I don't want to look at her, but she asks me so sweetly to do so that I cannot resist.

"Why are you being so stubborn, cousin?"

I don't answer. I wipe my mouth on the sleeve of my shirt and see blood dirty it further.

"Sweet, sweet, Kai. I have always loved you the most of all my family."

"Just go if you are going to try to convince me to say anything about any of this." I feel the sting of a tear as it leaves my eye.

"I know you too well to assume I can talk you into anything." She strokes the side of my face. "You must really love her."

Another tear escapes me.

"There is to be a feast this evening. We will all be there. Eating, and drinking. Oh, we will be drinking so very much." She glances toward the door to the cell. "If you were to get free of your restraints and wait for an hour after nightfall, you could be long gone before anyone knows what happened."

I stare at her, studying her face. She keeps pushing her long, straight hair out of her face and appears genuinely distraught.

"Your father believes that Rachel Hart is General Grayson's granddaughter. And Old Man Grayson is not stable." She smiles sweetly before holding up a single-sided razor. Black tape is wrapped around all sides except the sharpest. "Promise me you will live a long and loving life."

We both jump when we hear voices just outside the door. She holds the razor close to my lips and says, "Hide this."

I take the blade into my mouth and feel the sharp prick as I use my tongue to work it to the inside of my cheek.

"I love you, cousin," Camryn says. "Buon viaggio."

Safe travels.

She is at the door, opening it, when Jonas comes in.

"Any luck?" he asks her.

"None." She hesitates at the door. "You will join me for dinner tonight?"

I hear disgust in her voice but know Jonas is too ignorant to catch it.

"Yes, I will be right there."

She leaves the door open. Jonas glances at it as he stands just inches from me.

"You are disgusting," he says. He grabs me by the throat and the jolting of my head causes the razor to dig into the side of my tongue. "I hope he lets me be the one to slit your throat tomorrow. The best part? Your execution will be a public affair. My dick grows hard just thinking about watching you bleed to death."

I want to spit on him but know blood is pooling in my mouth and if he sees it he will know something is going on. I squeeze my eyes shut to block him out.

"Jonas," Camryn calls out to him from somewhere not too far away.

He pulls his attention back to me.

"Get ready to die, you little bitch." He lets go of my neck and laughs. "Enjoy your last night of life." Then he is gone.

I need to begin my plan for escape but the pain in my full bladder is becoming too much to take. I try to pull myself up but the pressure low in my abdomen is a hindrance. Choosing freedom over dignity, I soil my pants with urine.

I work the razor blade around in my mouth until the cutting edge faces out, then clamp my teeth onto it. Pulling my body up causes the ropes to cut roughly into my wrists, but I must do this now.

I use a back and forth sawing motion with the razor against the rope located on the inside of my right hand. My shoulder is on fire and my arms ache, but I keep going. I cut at the portion of rope that will be out of sight if someone comes in to check on me.

The party must be in full swing since no one comes to my cell for a very long time.

Finally, I get my right hand free, and use it to grip the rope as I try to work my left hand from the rope. It is not long before I realize I will need to make a second cut to free my other hand. Every cell in my body screams in pain as I hang on.

I close my eyes and work the razor against the rope until I fall to the ground and land on the blade. The pain of the laceration barely registers over that of the earlier blows to my body. Blood oozes from my left forearm. But finally, there is relief for my shoulder.

I gather the blade and damaged rope in an attempt to hide the assistance I received. There is blood on the floor, but I do not worry about that. My only concern with the laceration is that I do not leave a blood trail for the soldiers to follow. I use the blade to cut off the sleeve of my shirt, tie that around my injury, and go to the door.

I listen. Wait. When I am confident that I hear nothing, I open the door and peer out. There is no one around.

I run for my life. Once again I am in the position that my mission is to stay alive.

The tunnel is utterly dark and panic rises in me with every step. I strain my eyes trying to see. What if this is a setup? Who is waiting outside of the tunnel to ambush me? I've never before felt trapped inside this mountain, but I am having trouble breathing and know it isn't only from my exertion.

Rachel, Rachel, Rachel, I chant in my head, her name keeping time with my steps. I have to make it back to Rachel to warn her that they are looking for her.

When I emerge into the shadowy darkness outside, I look for the moon. It's barely a sliver, but by its position above the familiar group of three boulders, I guess it's about nine o'clock. My father's people should be partying for several more hours. Maybe I will get a good enough head start to escape them after all.

Still grasping the rope and razor, I run. I sprint down the dusty path. I run past the first stand of trees and head toward the second. My abdomen screams at me, still feeling the blows from Jonas.

My feet feel the impact with every step. I will surely have blisters, I think, then laugh at myself for believing any of it will matter if I don't get far, far away.

I keep running, even though the ground crumbles beneath my weary feet, even though I am sliding on the dry leaves that await the torrential rains that will soon come and grind them into the ground, enriching the newly rehydrated earth. I keep running, clumsily, fiercely.

Stumbling, I know I cannot keep sprinting like this. I won't last long at this pace. Forcing myself, I slow to a jog and work to steady my breathing. Then I concentrate on the sounds around me. All I hear is my breathing and my footfalls. I will need to keep aware of my surroundings, keep aware that my father's soldiers might try to follow me back to the others.

The pain from my booted feet worsens. My abdomen hurts. But still I move forward. *Rachel*!

I no longer possess the rope or razor and have no idea when I dropped them. I no longer care. To my left is where I bedded down with Rachel that one night. Before she was *my* Rachel, when she was so very angry with me. I imagine making love to her there sometime in the future. This is just what I need to inspire me to keep going.

Smoke drifts on a current of air. Knowing it is probably a soldier checkpoint, I step off the trail slightly. I am downwind so luck might be on my side and maybe they won't hear me. I go farther off the trail, and soon I am losing my footing, sliding halfway down the embankment, but I am miraculously still on my feet. I move quickly, carefully picking my way along the forest floor. My legs are like rubber and, if I stop the forward movement, I may never get going again.

I no longer smell smoke and believe I am beyond the checkpoint. Hopefully the soldiers are night-sleepy and have no idea of my presence. I climb up the dried creek bed, and when I return to the main path, it is dark and eerily quiet.

I pick up my pace again. My throat is raw and my vision is blurred. Breathing is getting harder and harder. I feel wounds on my feet deepening with every step. I want to slow down to a walk, but I'm pretty sure if I stop running I will fall. My legs are barely holding me up, but I must keep going.

The next time I am really aware of my surroundings, the sky is streaked with orange, red, and pink. By now my father and the soldiers surely know I have fled.

Blood pounds in my ears, making me desperate and dizzy.

Soon, I approach the place where I can veer off to the east and be at Karst in just a few hours. Suzanna would take me into her arms, she would feed me toast and tea, and would tell me it was okay that I chose my life over continuing on to find the others.

Or I can take the path to the west and go find Rachel. She needs to know she is in danger. This exercise of weighing my options is just that, an exercise, because I already know there is no choice to be made. I will go to Rachel. Or die trying.

†

When I fall I do not have the strength to get back up. Inside I am wailing against this failure of mine. I have let Rachel down. I have not made it back to her to warn her.

I feel fat drops of rain on my face and wonder if I'm hallucinating. Images play against the inside of my eyelids. I see Rachel across the dining hall and imagine she looks at me with desire. I am making love to her at Karst and cannot believe how amazing it feels to be touched like that, by her.

I dream about the coywolf, Ajax, with his soulful eyes and dark muzzle. I dream that he comes to ease my death, his hot breath on my neck as he nudges me, urging me. Then he is gone and I am alone again, alone in my failure, rain hitting my face. And now I must be dead, as the most gorgeous goddess or angel or collection of particles is looking down into my face and smiling. *Rachel*.

When I awaken, I am on Shakespeare's back with Rachel. She holds me up from behind, her arms wrapped around me. I feel her lips soft against my ear; her words are gentle puffs of air.

"My love."

I rest into her embrace, the side-to-side rocking motion of the shiny black horse beneath me. My eyes burn with unshed tears. The relief that flows over me is threatening to overwhelm.

"Rachel," I whisper.

"Yes?"

I have told everyone but Rachel about my love for her. I break down with that thought, horrified that I might have died without telling her.

"I love you."

"I know, my sweet. I love you, too."

Gotham rides up beside us.

"Ah, welcome back to the living, Kai."

I give him a weak smile. Content to be there in Rachel's arms, I close my eyes again until our forward movement ceases.

"Are we stopping?" I ask her.

"Yes, love." She kisses the side of my head. "We are stopping for the night."

"Did I miss the rain?" I ask, still not feeling quite myself.

"Yes, sweetheart, it rained a little."

Gotham and Jackson help me down off Shakespeare. They settle me against a boulder and I see that my feet have already been tended to. I look around for Rachel, hoping she will join me. Instead, it is Dr. Bradshaw who comes to sit beside me.

"Hey, Doc, when did you get out here?"

"Right after you were taken. Suzanna relented, soon after your party left, and allowed me to come out here in case I was needed. Luke escorted me." She smiles sweetly at me. "Apparently, I am needed out here."

I nod. I glance around and marvel that our numbers have swelled yet again.

"Is there anything about your injuries that I should know?" the doctor asks.

"No. Just some blows to the body and face." I know she is asking if I've been sexually assaulted again. I glance down at my feet. "And I guess some blisters."

"I am glad you didn't suffer anything else. But your feet are in bad shape. It looks like you ran for many miles on very little of your boots. There was no sole left on one when we found you, and the other boot consisted of just the top tied to your foot." She squeezes my hand. "Are you okay— emotionally?"

"My father was preparing for my public execution. Emotionally—I don't know what to do with that." I look up as Breanne comes closer. She and Rachel keep their distance, giving me my privacy with Dr. Bradshaw.

"There are things I need to discuss with my sister," I say.

"Of course. I will redress your feet before we head out in the morning. Have someone carry you when you need to go relieve yourself and when you go bed down for the night. I don't want you putting any weight on your feet yet." She smiles and adds, "I'm so glad you are back with us."

"Thank you."

Breanne and Rachel approach me at the same time. Rachel looks shy and offers to leave so Breanne and I can have some time alone, but I tell her that I want her to stay, that I have something I need to tell them both.

"Maybe Gotham can come over and hear this as well?" I ask.

Breanne calls Gotham over to join us.

I tell them about the questions Father wanted answered. That even though he was keen on knowing where my siblings were, he was more interested in finding Rachel.

"He knew her real last name," I say, fully aware that this is the first time I've ever come close to telling anyone else that Rachel's last name is Hart.

"Which is?" Breanne asks.

I don't want to answer, so I stall. "He said they only want her for a DNA test. I learned from Camryn that it is to see if she is the granddaughter of General Grayson."

Rachel gasps.

"Are you?" Gotham turns to Rachel.

"I do not know my father's name."

"But?" Breanne chimes in.

"But he was a guard at ND3 when my mother was a prisoner there. All I know is that he raped her, but then departed shortly after I was born."

"What is your mother's name?" Breanne asks Rachel.

She looks at me. I cannot tell her who to trust, and with how much. She must decide this for herself now.

"My mother's name was Hannah Hart."

"Is Rachel your real name?" Gotham asks.

"Yes. My name is Rachel Hart," she whispers. "I am the daughter of an Anointed prisoner and Resistance soldier."

She looks so lost that I cannot help myself. I pull her down to where I sit and embrace her.

"Rachel Hart, only we need to know your name. You are still Rachel Prince to everyone else." Breanne kneels down in front of us.

Rachel nods.

"Does Grayson just want what's his returned to him, or is there another reason he is trying to identify his granddaughter?" Breanne asks.

I shrug. I am feeling so tired and just want to hold Rachel in my arms until I fall asleep.

"Father didn't say anything that would lead you to guess what their endgame is?" Breanne asks.

"No. When I tried to ask him questions about the Hart woman he grew angry with me."

Breanne nods. Then she asks Rachel if she can have a moment with me. Gotham offers to help Rachel put together an evening meal for us. Once they are gone, Breanne tells me that Rachel tried to trade herself for me when the soldiers took me away.

"I tell you this because now we know that because of her feelings for you, Rachel cannot be trusted to follow the plan."

"I guess things are twice as bad as you think then, because I will break ranks for her as well. And for you, and Gotham."

"We cannot have all of this sentimentality, Kai. This isn't part of the plan." Breanne's nostrils flare slightly.

"Neither was my getting caught and ending up at ND3. Neither was having Rachel there to keep me alive." I refuse to back down on this. "And neither was my falling in love with her."

Breanne sighs. "When we topple father's dynasty—and we will do just that—is there anyone you would like us to have mercy on?"

"Yes, we must have mercy on Camryn."

"Then that will be so."

"But we can be particularly harsh with Jonas," I add.

"Indeed, that too is what we will do. What do you hear about Lewis?"

"Nothing. I have not laid eyes on him since before my time at ND3. The only sign that he exists is Father mentioning him, and seeing Sebastian at the homestead."

"Tell me about Sebastian."

"I believe he is lost to us. I hope I'm wrong, but he seems overly influenced by Father." I grow despondent as I say these words. I truly do hope I am wrong.

"That is too bad." She shrugs. "Eat. And rest. We'll talk more later." She holds out my gun and holster. "You did good hiding this."

I take my gear from her. When Breanne leaves me, I am rejoined by Rachel.

"Hungry?" Rachel asks.

"Very." I smile, then lean closer. "Hungry in more ways than one."

She holds my gaze. "I, too, want to be intimate. But mostly I am just so relieved that you are back with me. Where you belong," she adds shyly.

"Yes, with you is exactly where I belong."

We eat, then I have Jackson help me to the area where I am to relieve myself. He turns away until I tell him I am ready, then he carries me to my bedding.

"Sleep well," he says with a wink before leaving me there with Rachel.

Darkness descends and the air grows slightly cooler. I pull Rachel against me.

"I love you," I whisper into her ear.

"I love you, too."

"Can I touch you?" I ask.

"We are not basking in privacy here, you know." I can feel her smile against my lips.

"Just let me kiss your breasts, then I will behave." It is my turn to smile.

"Promise?"

"Promise to kiss your breasts or to behave?" I tease.

"Both."

"Yes." I pull the thin blanket over our heads and lift Rachel's shirt. When my lips find her nipple the jolt of pleasure it sends through me is amazing. She moans. I suck her nipple into my mouth and lash at it with my tongue. It feels so good to touch her, to feel her respond to me.

A soft groan escapes her. "Kai," she whispers.

I keep suckling on her breast, knowing I am not really keeping my promise, but I at least stay there at her breast and don't go lower, even though I hunger immensely for her wetness. I give her nipple one last, light kiss, then drift off to sleep.

CHAPTER TEN

In the morning when I awake, Rachel is watching me. Tears fall from her eyes, splashing onto my neck.

"What's wrong?" I ask.

"I can't stop thinking about how close I came to losing you." She sobs.

"I'm here. I'm fine. It's all okay."

She buries her face into my neck and I can tell by the jerking of her breaths that she is still crying.

"I will die if anything ever happens to you."

"Nothing's going to happen. And even if something did, you—"

"I can't do this," she says. "I can't take it, knowing that harm can come to you out here. Can't we go back to Karst?"

"You don't really want that, you're just scared, and that's okay. It's okay to be scared." I kiss her forehead.

"I do want that. I want to go back to Karst with you and make love to you all day and all night. I want to go to sleep at night without fearing for your safety."

I swallow against the lump in my throat. I cannot go back to Karst, not now, not until peace has been acquired. But I also can't keep her from going back if that's what she wants. "Luke is to leave later today to return to Karst. If you want to go with him I will understand."

"*We* can go back with him."

"No, I cannot. But it is perfectly fine if you want to." I stroke the side of her face. "I will understand if you want to leave."

"With you." She kisses me hard on the mouth before abruptly pulling away. "I want to leave with you. Only with you."

"I cannot go, Rachel. You know that."

Her tears flow and she has a moment of breathlessness.

"I do know that. But I can't stand the thought of losing you out here. I was so scared when the soldiers took you away. I thought I would die right then and there."

"But you didn't die, and I am fine, and it will be okay as long as we are together, as long as we love one another." I think about Suzanna saying something similar before we left Karst and miss her tremendously. I imagine that I smell rosemary.

Rachel slides her hand down between my legs. No one else is stirring yet around us, but it is still not private enough for us to make love in this beginning light.

"We can't," I say, but my hips have already started to respond to her touch and I know there is no going back now. I whisper, "Rachel."

She kisses me as her fingers smear through my wetness, catching my moans into her mouth, making every inch of me press upward, needing more and more of her touch. My release is intense and I hold her tightly as I cry into her neck. I don't want her to leave me but I will never ask her to stay.

When I finally stop shaking, Rachel whispers, "Please don't ever die on me, please don't let anything happen to you—ever. I am begging you."

"I'm here, sweetheart, I am here." I will not make a promise I cannot keep, but I will remind her that I am with her now. "We are together here."

People around us are beginning to stir. I sit up and watch Rachel for signs as to whether or not she has decided to leave.

"I will let Dr. Bradshaw know you are ready for her to rewrap your feet?"

I nod. I am afraid to ask if she will return to Karst with Luke or stay with me.

"I imagine we will be breaking camp and continuing on soon."

And there I have my answer.

Breakfast is eaten quickly, then Breanne calls Gotham, Jackson, and several others over to us. Rachel comes to stand at my side.

"Okay, listen up," Breanne says. "If Father's soldiers come, we will show no mercy, we will not bother to take anyone alive."

Everyone nods, but no one speaks. Rachel strokes the length of her bow.

"We will continue our journey to McNally, taking the final settlement quickly and without mercy. We must all be vigilant."

People are nodding, glancing around as if to show they have started their vigilance already.

We are breaking down camp when a group of people ride toward us. They are not in any singular uniform, but much like us, in miscellaneous, civilian clothing. We all stand and draw our weapons, including Rachel, who has her bow in front of her with an arrow at the ready, although pointing downward. I step slightly ahead of Rachel, out of instinct.

My heartbeat quickens when I recognize my brother, Lewis, as the lead horseback rider.

"Whoa," he says as he pulls up on his horse's reins. "It's me, Lewis."

"Exactly," Gotham says. "Drop your weapons. Everyone. One wrong move and we fire on the whole group of you."

"My only weapon is stowed away in my pack at the back of my horse." Lewis holds up his hands. He looks at me. "Kai. I am so glad to see you."

I don't respond. My emotions are so scattered that I don't know if I feel joy or fear over seeing Lewis.

With his hands still up, he uses pressure from his legs to ease his horse forward. He looks more closely at me.

"You have recently taken a beating?"

"What are you doing here, Lewis?" Breanne asks, her voice hard.

Lewis doesn't take his eyes off me. His gaze drifts down to my feet, still bandaged and not quite ready for boots.

"Are you okay?" he asks me. The way his voice catches in his throat makes my defenses falter for just a moment, then I remember he was always closest to Father. He nods his head toward one of my feet. "Where did that happen?"

"Ask your father," Gotham says through gritted teeth.

"At the homestead? With Father's consent?" Lewis asks.

Finally finding my voice, I say, "Yes, with General Brodie's consent. And under his order."

"I am here with a contingent of northern Isolationists. We intend to bring an end to Father's reign." Lewis lowers his arms and Gotham points the gun more fully at his head, causing Lewis to then raise his hands again.

"From where do you come?" Breanne asks.

A dark man rides a chestnut mare forward from the periphery of the pack. When he stops his forward movement, he clicks his tongue at the horse.

"We are mostly from Lutherville, but some are from Washington, and some from the midlands." He gestures to his leg. "I have a firearm but have no desire to use it on you. We have come to join the movement. We have come to fight for peace."

Now Lewis moves forward until he is even with the dark man.

"What is your name?" Breanne asks.

"I am John. John Stevens."

"Do we know yet what Father's plans are?" Lewis asks. "Does he plan to come after us?"

"Where have you been, Lewis?" I ask. All heads turn to look at me. "Where have you been and what have you been doing?"

"I have been looking for you." He stares at me as he speaks. "I hoped to find you well at ND3 but did not. No one I interviewed remembered anyone named Kai there. But you were there, weren't you?"

I do not respond.

His eyes dart to Rachel, then return to me.

"Where have you really been?" Breanne asks.

"After I could not find Kai at any of the detention centers, I went back to Lutherville." He turns to look behind him and gestures toward a woman on a horse. She rides up and I see something is strapped to her chest. "I made it back there just in time for the birth of my daughter."

I know in that instant that Lewis has fallen in love with this woman and will make sure that Father will never have a chance to influence his infant girl. I look at Breanne, then Gotham, and know they have not come as completely to that conclusion as I have.

Our people all match up with one of Lewis's and we strip them of their firearms. We find radios on several of them, and one has a tattoo scanner, all of which we also take from them before letting them come to the fire for a meal.

"Kai, you and Prince assist Jackson in preparing the grains and kudzu root," Breanne says. There seems to be a silent consensus. From then on, everyone calls Rachel by her registered last name. I am moved by this instant unity with the people we've been traveling with.

Rachel and I busy ourselves with meal preparation. Beside us, Shawn roasts a few rabbits.

When it is time to eat, Rachel and I join the others around the fire. I can't take my eyes off the woman Lewis is now coupled with. She is several shades lighter than my siblings and I, with light brown highlights in her dark brown hair. She catches my eye several times but then looks away shyly.

Lewis approaches us after we eat. Gotham stays close.

"Kai." My oldest brother looks softer than I've ever seen him. Is it the few pounds he seems to have gained, or is it this new love of his? "I am so thankful that you are okay."

He stares at Rachel. "I am Lewis Brodie," he says to Rachel as he extends his hand.

She takes his hand but says nothing.

"You are Rachel," he says, his voice barely over a whisper.

She reclaims her hand and steps back. I gently squeeze her shoulder. We are both rigid, and I'm pretty sure when Breanne approaches us it is because she has read our body language.

"Am I sensing some discomfort here?" Breanne asks.

"Lewis seems to think she is called Rachel," I say, my eyes boring into him as I answer Breanne.

"He does, does he?" Breanne squares her shoulders and moves closer, putting herself between Lewis and Rachel.

"I am friendly with Rachel Hart's father, Sergeant Thomas Grayson."

Breanne's hand is on her sidearm.

"Whoa," Lewis says. "Thomas is not like his father—or ours."

Her hand remains on her weapon. "Why are you here, Lewis?"

"I have come with a message for Rachel Hart." His eyes flick to Rachel, then return to Breanne. "Thomas desires an opportunity to meet his daughter. No strings attached, no expectations, just the chance to have a few moments with her."

"Why would you expect us to believe that is all you have come for? Or that he deserves a meeting with anyone? Or that he is this Rachel Hart person's father?" Breanne asks.

I appreciate that she still hasn't let on that we know anything about a Rachel Hart. I look at my brother and his expression makes me believe he knows already that my Rachel Prince is also Rachel Hart.

"My mission is twofold. First, to get Thomas's message to his daughter. And second, I wish to band with the Peace Movement and bring an end, finally, to all of the oppression from both the Resistance and the Anointed."

"Why should we trust you?" I ask.

"I have grown so weary of the army life," Lewis says as he shakes his head. "I no longer trust the Resistance Army. I am ready to be on the right side of history."

"Your contingent—are they here for Thomas or for Peace?"

"They are here for Peace. I am the only one trying to do a favor for a friend."

Gotham approaches.

"What is going on over here that has everyone looking so very serious?"

"Our big brother has it in his head that Prince is really Rachel Hart, and that his friend, Sergeant Thomas Grayson, is her father." Breanne keeps her eyes locked on Lewis as she speaks to Gotham.

"Interesting. And why is he here?" Gotham asks.

"To deliver a message from Thomas to Rachel, and to join the Peace Movement," Lewis says, holding Breanne's gaze instead of looking at Gotham.

"And how do we feel about that?" Gotham asks.

"Distrustful," I answer. "And weary."

"And what do we do about this?" Gotham continues.

"What *do* we do?" Breanne counters.

"We keep moving forward, keep growing our numbers, and when we approach the juncture with the route to Thomas, you decide if you want me to go for him." Lewis looks at me as he speaks.

"Why should we waste any time or thought on Thomas Grayson?" Gotham asks.

"To get answers," Lewis says. "And just for humoring him he will give you access to some helpful technology. What have you got to lose?"

"Time. Resources," Breanne says.

"If you don't trust me to send for Thomas, then you can go to him."

"It could be a trap." Breanne crosses her arms over her chest as she speaks. "But I suppose we could consider sending one or two people."

"Surely you don't mean *expendable* people," Gotham says, his voice low and barely heard.

"Surely not," Breanne says, her voice sounding impatient.

"I will go then," Gotham says.

"No, I will go." I step forward as I say this.

"No way, Kai is *not* going," Gotham says, looking at Breanne.

"We don't need to make a decision about this yet," Breanne says.

Lewis nods and then looks at me. I do not look away, nor do I respond, knowing the decision is Breanne's to make, as far as moving forward with Lewis and his people.

"We need to be moving soon. How many days' provisions do you carry?" Breanne asks.

"We are good for seven to ten days if we are smart about it."

"You will need every bit of that if you plan to come with us." Breanne looks over to where Lewis's lover breastfeeds the infant. "It is dangerous for the child to be out here with us."

"It was more dangerous for her not to be." Lewis crosses his arms over his chest in a way that tells me he anticipated the remark. "I will protect my family with my life. And by family I mean all of it—wife, baby, and siblings."

I believe him at that moment. How can I not?

"We will all travel together then. If at any time I feel like you are playing us, I will kill you myself," Breanne says.

Surprise is evident on Lewis's face, but he nods in understanding. Apparently he hasn't seen this side of Breanne before. I can't help but smile.

Our hodge-podge of warriors is swelling in size, more and more every day. I look around and feel the urgency—and the desire to make New America safe for everyone—and am amazed that all these different people have come together for the greater good.

†

We've been on the move for two days when Lewis shows us on a map where the settlement managed by Sergeant Thomas Grayson is located. It is on the other side of the dry bed of the Black River. To get to the easiest crossing point, the battered remains of the city of Ellenton must be traversed.

"If we determine it best to not go through Ellenton, then it will be another day's travel to get to a different crossing point," Lewis says.

"Tell us about the Black River," Gotham says.

"It is dry now, but in the blink of an eye the black waters can rush down and turn it into a raging beast. When this happens, it takes several days before the water is low—and slow—enough to cross with horses."

"So the person who goes across the riverbed could get stuck over there for days." Breanne is deep in thought as she speaks. "So it's still best that only a few people go."

After some deliberation between Breanne and Gotham, it is determined that on the following day a small contingent will go through Ellenton, but only one person is to cross the riverbed. Lewis has told us about the remains of a bridge that is deep within the city. It is a two-foot wide section that spans the entire riverbed, is in decent shape, and can be traveled by foot as long as the wind isn't too strong.

"Other than Rachel, I have the most to lose where anything to do with her is concerned. I want to be the one to cross the riverbed." I stand as tall as I can on my still-sore feet as I say this.

Gotham looks as if to protest, when Breanne agrees.

"Yes, it should be Kai who goes."

"It will be dangerous," Gotham says. "We know nothing about this man or his people."

Sergeant Grayson might take me prisoner, he might hand me over to my father, or he might have me tortured and killed. But I will risk all of that if it means figuring out how I can better protect my love.

Breanne studies Lewis for several minutes. "Tell us why we should trust the safety of any of us where Thomas Grayson is concerned."

"If Thomas wasn't so preoccupied with finding his daughter, he would have joined the Peace Movement long before now. He is a good man. I can vouch for him. And I can go with the chosen contingent if you'd like." Lewis looks at me as he says this, a tenderness on his face that surprises me.

"No, what I would like," Breanne says, "is for you to stay here with us. You will serve as insurance. If anything happens to Kai at Sergeant Grayson's hands, you will pay with your life."

She turns to look at Lewis's wife and infant. "What is your wife's name?"

"Cora. My wife is Cora and my baby is Daphne."

"If any harm comes to Kai during this mission to see Thomas Grayson, you will watch the death of Cora and Daphne before you are executed. Do you understand this?" Breanne asks, her voice hard.

"As you wish." If Lewis is surprised, he hides it well.

I wait until we are bedding down to ask Rachel how she feels about the prospect of meeting her father.

"I'm nervous," she whispers. "If Thomas Grayson is indeed my father, I would like to know it."

"If he is and can prove it, will you agree to meet him?" I ask.

She is quiet for a long time.

"I don't know. I don't think I will know until that time comes," she says finally.

"That's fair enough." I wrap my arms around her and pull her close. "No matter what you decide, you have my full support."

"I know. Thank you." She kisses my cheek, then my mouth.

"I love you."

"I love you, too. Now go to sleep. You need your rest for tomorrow."

†

Breanne lectures me before I leave, reminding me that I have a role to play in the greater movement for peace, beyond my relationship with Rachel. I do not contradict her, even though I know that everything outside of Rachel is inconsequential to me.

"Your mission is to find Thomas Grayson and determine if he is friend or foe, whether it is reasonable that he might be Rachel's father, and whether or not he is worthy of joining us. You are to decide how he should be dealt with."

"I understand," I say as I nod.

"Do you? You will need to dig deep and make some extremely important decisions. Your first instinct will be to make things as easy as possible for Rachel. But that might not be the best thing for her—or for us."

"I do understand."

"You accept this mission and all the responsibility it includes?" Breanne asks, watching me.

"I accept."

She places a hand on my shoulder.

"I really am impressed with the woman you have become, Kai, and I want to have you around for a very long time. Please be careful."

"I will. I have so much to come back to." I smile at my sister, then turn as Rachel approaches.

"You are almost ready?" Rachel asks.

"Yes." I draw her to the side and pull her into an embrace. "I will see you soon."

"Can't someone else go?" she asks into my neck.

"We've already talked about this." I pull away just far enough to kiss her mouth lightly. "Everything will be fine."

Gotham approaches and I release Rachel. He pulls me into a rough hug.

"Safe travels, little sister."

Lewis hesitates before approaching me.

"We have the radios if you wish to communicate with us." He turns to Gotham. "Well, that is you have the radios. Maybe Kai should take one with her."

Breanne nods and gets one of the radios she confiscated from Lewis's men out of her pack.

"Have Lewis show you how to use this."

It only takes a few minutes for my lesson with the radio. Then Lewis tells me I should ask Thomas for a fully charged battery to bring back after my meeting with him.

I mount a mare named Firefall and envision all the ways to make this mission a success. Once I have visualized my safe passage across the riverbed, I squeeze the horse with my legs. I look one last time at Rachel, give her a smile, and encourage Firefall to move forward.

Lewis's friend John Stevens, Nell, and two of Breanne's longtime warriors come with me to Ellenton.

I pause before following the crumbled road into the city. Ajax has come this far with us, but I don't feel good about him coming into the city.

"Go back," I tell the coywolf.

I hear a sharp whistle from where we left the others, then a coywolf yelp I know to be Gotham.

"Go," I say, waving my hand.

Ajax retreats and I am relieved.

Stevens knows the city, has picked his way through the rubble more than once. We follow his lead around long-dead and mangled powerlines, structures in varying levels of ruin, and large craters where bombs from distant enemies slammed into the city so long ago. A few structures' walls remain; some are inches high, others several feet. None of the structures can be saved, they would need to be razed to rebuild this place. This is obviously a city that no one has tried to bring back to life with churches or prisons.

I am impressed with the care Stevens takes of the horses as he traverses this dangerous landscape. Suzanna's words come to me and I hear her quoting someone from many lifetimes ago, about how a society is only as good as how it treats its animals.

When we arrive at the riverbed, I am surprised by how wide it is, but its blackness surprises me even more.

"The water comes from beyond the scorched land in the North, and brings the soot with it. The riverbed is black from the sooty sediment that stays behind," Stevens explains.

We both look to the North.

"The clouds continue to build and the rains continue to fall in the North."

I nod in understanding, then look at what remains of the bridge and try to imagine how impressive the bridge must have looked when it was intact. I hope I can ride Firefall in both directions and not end up having to use what is left of the bridge to come back across.

I take one last look at my companions and then coax my horse to begin the crossing. I am careful of debris that litters the riverbed, parts of rusted old cars, chunks of buildings, and other things that I cannot identify from the world before my time.

As we begin the gradual ascent up the opposite bank of the river, I grip Firefall just a little tighter with my legs. I relax slightly as we start across the level ground.

I ride for a couple of miles before I see signs of the settlement. Within minutes of knowing I have arrived, I see two sentries point their rifles at me as I approach. I stop

Firefall when I am within a few yards of them and raise my hands.

"I am unarmed."

"Who are you and why do you trespass?" a curly-haired man asks.

"I am here to seek an audience with Thomas Grayson."

"And why should Sergeant Grayson speak with you?"

"Lewis Brodie has sent me."

"What is your business?"

"I wish to discuss Rachel Hart with the Sergeant," I say as my heart pounds in my chest.

The second man speaks into a radio, too low for me to hear his words.

I am told to get off the mare and to lead her alongside me. Within minutes I'm flanked by soldiers. One pats me down and nods when he is convinced I am not armed.

"Come this way," he says.

There are what must be motorbikes zipping around, a sight I never imagined seeing in real life, but about which I have heard stories. They appear—and sound—just as I've heard them described by elders at Karst. This will be something worth testifying about over a fire in Karst, with Suzanna and the others. Assuming I make it back to the others, that is, and then back to Karst after peace has been won.

I am led into a lightly guarded fortress. There are antennas and towers everywhere. I look up and wonder if the communication towers are how they transmit the data from the tattoo readers. Half of what I see I have no idea of its name or its use. The rooftops are all covered in solar panels, much bigger ones than I've seen at our homestead, near Karst, or at ND3.

Only a few of the soldiers are armed. Most of the people inside the complex are not dressed like soldiers. They are clean and carry themselves in a most relaxed manner.

The building I am brought to is well lit and immaculate. I enter a room with desks and what I believe to be computers throughout it. I feel like I have walked into a parallel universe. I glance down at my clothing and feel dirty, primitive.

I take a step closer to one of the machines on a desk.

"Have you seen a computer before?" a man's voice asks. "Go closer if you wish."

I startle, then calm down when I see him across the room. His questioning smile, slightly amused by me, reminds me of Rachel's when I first saw her as a guard. He is standing at a long table and bows slightly.

"Welcome to our outpost. I am Thomas Grayson." He extends his hand but I do not take it. I also do not introduce myself yet. He pulls back his hand and continues. "You are here on Lewis Brodie's behalf, I understand."

"Yes."

"You come with word of Rachel Hart?"

I do not answer.

"Please," he gestures to a chair across the table from him. "Sit. Make yourself comfortable. Can I get you something to drink?"

"No, thank you." I sit as he requests.

"Do you know my daughter personally?"

I am sizing him up in lieu of answering him. He is younger than my own father. And taller.

"Please, is she well?" he asks.

It can't hurt to at least tell him that she is fine, right?

"I am not at liberty to tell you anything specific about the woman you are assuming is your daughter," I start out by saying.

"But she's okay?"

"Yes, she is fine."

He closes his eyes briefly, then opens them. "Thank you." His words sound so sincere.

I look at him and the resemblance to Rachel is unmistakable, despite his hair being a bit darker than hers. I will not admit this to him.

"Why do you send soldiers after her?"

"That sounds harsh. I have only sent scouts out looking for her."

"You have enlisted General Brodie to find her—at any cost."

"I have done no such thing." He leans slightly forward and stares at me. "That man is to stay away from her!"

I am confused by his reaction.

He takes a deep breath, presumably to settle his anger.

"General Brodie and I do not see eye to eye on the direction the Resistance should take. He's calling for a final solution to the Anointed, and I—well, I believe mercy for both sides should be shown on a case-by-case basis."

"You are not in agreement with the Resolution?"

"No, I am not." His brows knit together.

"So why does he want your daughter?"

"Leverage. He wants her as leverage." He sighs. "He thinks if he has her he can keep me in line. My men and I control the technology and have the knowledge to use it most effectively."

"Why should I believe you?"

"I can't answer that for you. If you've ever met General Brodie or his thugs, you'd know how reprehensible—"

"But," I interrupt him, "why should *I* believe *you*?"

"Because I am willing to let you walk out of here with a message for her. You can leave at any time. I will give you safe passage."

"Why?"

"So you can tell her I would like to see her—to talk to her."

"Why?" I again ask.

"Because after years of thinking she was killed alongside her mother, I have been assured that she survived after all."

"And after what you did to her mother—"

"I was not in control of that."

"Any man who uses that as an excuse should be castrated!" I jump to my feet. "You are an animal."

Now he is standing.

"I beg your pardon! You were not there—you did not see me dragged out of there—"

"Good thing I didn't see you rape that poor woman. I would have slit your throat right then and there."

"What?" He stumbles backward a step.

Two armed men rush in. Grayson holds out his hands, then says to them, "Stand down."

My anger mixes with my own confusion.

The other men leave the room and Grayson turns back to me.

"What did you say?"

"You raped Rachel's mother, then moved on to your next post." My hands curl into fists at my sides.

"I was in love with Hannah Hart. I was going to sneak her out of there and we were going to raise our child together, up in Lutherville, hidden among the peaceful people there." Tears form in his eyes.

Now I hold his gaze, noticing how much his eyes are like Rachel's. Their color may be a slightly darker shade of amber than hers, but their shape and expression are the same. I find myself wondering if his eyes turn more golden in the sunlight like Rachel's, if at other times there are copper flecks in them. I have no doubt that he is Rachel's father, but I do doubt whether he is to be trusted.

He sits back onto his chair, roughly, with a thud.

"My superior made me leave ND3 soon after Rachel was born. I was sent to my father's post, and kept close to him, where I pretended to be assimilating back into a soldier's life outside of the detention system. All the while I planned how I was going to get Hannah and Rachel out of that hell."

I too sit.

"What happened next?" I ask, wondering if his story will match the little that Rachel knows of her own history.

"The Anointed rose up." He takes a deep breath. "There was a riot when they came to liberate their people from ND3. And Hannah—Hannah—" Thomas sobs. "I was told that she and the child died in the fighting."

I stare at him. His grief feels so real. I want to believe him—I want to think that Rachel has someone who has missed her all these years.

"Why do you now think that Rachel is alive?"

"I took possession of a man who was once a guard at ND3. While he was incarcerated at my post he told me things about the prison. He told me of some horrendous treatment by the guards, and he told me of some acts of beautiful mercy by others. When he mentioned Rachel by name…" he looks like he's left me mentally, and sits motionless for several moments, then says, "I knew in my heart that my daughter was alive."

Acts of beautiful mercy… the words swirl around in my head and I hope with all of my heart that this man is who and what he says he is, and that Rachel will know the love of her father, finally, after all these years.

"I went to ND3 with the liberators. No one knew where Rachel was, or they wouldn't tell me. So, I came back here and checked all the data of people coming out of ND3. I saw a Rachel Prince registered as property to a Brodie and I knew that was her." He narrows his eyes and grasps the edge of the table in front of him. "Wait. Are you Kai Brodie? You are General Brodie's daughter? You *own* my daughter?"

"Do not expect things to always be as they appear," I say, keeping my voice steadier than I feel.

"She is okay?" he asks, his voice breaking. "She is safe?"

"You have the technology for DNA testing here at this settlement?" I ask.

"Not quite. I've been trying to set up a lab here but have a few items missing yet. Grover is the only place I know with everything we need for that testing."

"I will take a sample of your blood back to my people and we will go to Grover."

"It will not stay viable long enough for you to do that. Both Rachel and I would need to be closer to Grover when our blood is drawn." He leans forward. "I will cross the riverbed with you."

"No."

"But—"

"That is not in the plan," I interrupt him. "You stay here, I will take this information back to my camp."

"I will see you again, though, right?" He sounds desperate.

"I give you my word." I stand.

"I have a new radio I can give you—so you can keep in touch. If you need me to come to you, just say so and I will." He also stands.

"Okay." I will take the radio and if Breanne decides it might be dangerous to have, I will be rid of it. "Please don't let any of your people follow me. One signal from me, and the others are long gone. If I don't make it back today by nightfall, you will be attacked by a force so deadly no person here will survive to utter your name."

He nods, not really convincing me that he has fallen for my bluff.

"I will get that radio. Travel safely."

†

I am not yet in sight of the riverbed when I hear the rushing of the water. I already know I am too late to make the crossing on horseback. I wiggle my feet in my boots and decide I will be able to cross what is left of the bridge by foot. I hate to leave my horse behind, but have no reason not to expect her to be well taken care of by Thomas Grayson's people.

I hear the engines of the motorbikes behind me. They approach slowly. Thomas and two of his men stop the bikes several yards away, presumably to keep from scaring my horse.

Thomas dismounts the bike and walks up to me.

"We can take the motorbikes across the bridge. It is how we cross when the river is up. Or, you can make yourself

209

comfortable for a few days—or a week—there's really no way to know for sure."

"I can walk across the remains of the bridge," I say.

"I noticed you limping earlier. The span of bridge that remains is not as easy as you might think. There's a section with questionable integrity."

"Bringing you back across with me was not in the plan," I remind him, and myself.

"You can't very well stop me," he says, a sly smile playing at the corners of his mouth. "It will be just me and one of my men. We will go unarmed, as you have come to us."

"And my horse?"

"Leave her here until later when the water recedes, and take the motorbike instead," he says as he gestures toward a bike ridden by a long-haired soldier.

I know I cannot keep him from driving his machines over the bridge, and that he would find the others long before me if he does.

"I will need you to show me that you are both unarmed. And how to use that thing," I add, pointing to the motorbike.

Thomas smiles and I see so much of my Rachel in his expression that it nearly takes my breath away.

Aaron, the soldier who will accompany Thomas and me, shows me how to operate the motorbike. He explains the fuel cells attached to the back of the bike. They have me drive it around for a little bit of practice before we start across the bridge.

"There is one section where the concrete is unstable. It is right after you crest the highest part of the structure. The trick is to keep up a good pace and use that momentum to fly over that section." He comes closer to me and extends his hand. "Please take care as you cross. I am looking forward to getting to know you better."

I feel a little nervous in my stomach at what he says, but hide it.

"There is nothing to worry about. I will make it safely across," I say.

"Aaron will cross first, then you, and I will be last."

I wonder if Aaron is the sacrificial lamb, sent over to test our forces on the other side.

We begin to cross the river on what is left of the bridge. The rumble of the motorbike's engine under me is a strange sensation. I attempt to keep my nerves in check and the machine on a steady course.

After Aaron has jumped the section of concern, Thomas shouts over the noise of the engines for me to start my ascent. The bike stays steady as I drive up the incline at the base. I will need to keep my speed up and my eyes on the route.

I am gripping the handlebars so tightly that my arms begin to ache. I am about to loosen my grasp when I see I am quickly approaching the section of missing concrete. I force myself to increase my speed and resist the temptation to glance down at the raging river below.

My legs extend and I lift off the seat of the motorbike, shifting my weight slightly, just as the concrete disappears. The roar of both the engine and the river fills my head as I soar across the crumbling span of bridge below me. When I land I use my legs to cushion the impact and maintain control over the motorbike, just as I might when jumping with a horse. Then I am on the decline leading to the other side of the wide riverbed. I exhale hard and find a small smile forming on my lips.

I did it.

I pull up beside Aaron and am warmed by the size of the smile on his face.

"Nicely done," he says.

I smile back and turn off my engine, as he has already done, and wait for Thomas.

When we ride into the heart of Ellenton, we are met by Stevens, Nell, and two others. Their horses are uneasy with the motorbikes. It is suggested that we stash the machines here in the city for the return trip across the riverbed. We lean them against a three-foot high section of wall, not really trying to hide them since people don't generally travel through Ellenton, but just having them together and available for later. We double up on the horses to ride through the remainder of the rubble of Ellenton.

The energy in the air is palpable as we ride into camp. I scan the crowd until I find Rachel. When our eyes meet, the smile that forms on her face embraces every inch of me. The horse I am on has barely stopped when I dismount and make my way toward her. When I come within ten feet of her, I halt.

I turn back and see Thomas and Aaron being frisked by my comrades. I gesture for Rachel to meet me over toward the sleeping area. I don't want her to have to deal with Thomas Grayson until she is ready.

Jackson, Breanne, Gotham, and a few others merge to form a wall between Grayson and where I stand with Rachel. I pull my lover into my arms and kiss her.

"I'm glad you are back," she whispers into my neck.

"I am glad as well." I pull away enough to look into her eyes. I see the eyes she shares with Thomas Grayson, and wonder if I should tell her my belief that he is indeed her father, or if I should wait until she asks for my opinion.

"You were treated well?" she asks.

"Yes, as a guest would be." I glance over to where Lewis is greeting Thomas and watch as they embrace.

"Welcome, my friend," I hear Lewis say.

Breanne approaches Rachel and me.

"When you are ready. Take as long as you need, and know that you do not have to speak with him if you do not want to," she says to my lover.

"I am ready." Rachel squares her shoulders and lifts her chin slightly.

Thomas and Lewis sit opposite me and Rachel around the fire, with Breanne, Lewis, Gotham, and Shelton separating us. Shawn stands a few feet behind Breanne, wound so tight that I am sure if Thomas even looks at Breanne wrong, Shawn will rip him to pieces.

"I am so happy to see you healthy," Thomas starts out.

Rachel does not respond.

Thomas takes a deep breath and grips a knee in each hand.

Rachel stares at him and I wonder if she sees herself in his face.

"I loved both you and your mother so very much," he says.

Rachel looks away now, her eyes resting somewhere past the man claiming to be her father.

For several moments Thomas is ignored.

"Is that so hard to believe?" He looks from me to her and back again. "Really? Why don't you tell me *your* love story? Which came first for you? Did you fall in love with Kai while you were her guard, or while you were her property?"

Rachel appears to deflate beside me and I put my arm around her shoulder. When I glance at Breanne she gives me a reassuring look and I just pull Rachel a little closer to me.

"Tell us some details of your time with Hannah Hart," Breanne says to Thomas.

He is looking at Rachel, but considering his faraway expression, I am willing to bet he's seeing Hannah.

"We started stealing glances at one another first, then moments of nearness. I will never forget the way she smiled when our eyes would meet across the garden. I was meant to be watching all of the women as they picked produce but I could never look away from her."

"I remember working in the garden with her when I was very young," Rachel says. "I don't believe I was accomplishing much, but I did a pretty good job of staying out of everyone's way."

"I was gone before you would have been old enough to go to the garden." He wipes away a tear and looks at Rachel until she looks up to meet his eyes. "My transfer came in the middle of the night, with no warning, and no time to say goodbye."

"And you never tried to get word to her?" Rachel asks.

"I was kept on a short leash for years after that." He stares into the fire, appearing far away. "One day you fell and hit the edge of the bunk, and oh your mother was absolutely frantic. It was just a little v-shaped cut on your—" He stops speaking when Rachel's fingers go to the scar under her chin.

"You have a scar there," he whispers, tears forming.

"Did the other guards know you were my father?"

Thomas's breath seems to catch in his chest. I know this is the point where it becomes clear to Rachel that Thomas is indeed her father. I had known for sure when I saw Thomas's eyes in the sunlight. The look on Rachel's face confirms she knows without a doubt now as well.

"Some knew, but not all," Thomas says. He shifts his body slightly. "There's a lab at the hospital in Grover where we can have a DNA test if that would help you to know definitively. We can have samples delivered to Grover without either of us needing to go there. We just need to be closer to the hospital when we draw the blood."

Rachel looks at me. I know by her expression that she wants to know what I think, but I cannot decide this for her.

"That would take us off course," she says as she looks back to Thomas.

Breanne has been staying mostly in the background up to this point, but now places a hand on Rachel's shoulder.

"If it brings you peace of mind we can go toward Grover so you can have your proof."

"May I please have a moment with Kai and Breanne?" Rachel asks Thomas.

Thomas nods and goes over to wait with Lewis and Cora. The others drift off to the side, out of hearing range.

"You think it's obvious he's my father, don't you?" she asks us both.

"In the end, the biology might not be the answer," Breanne says. "You can have proof he's your father and still not know if he has your best interest in mind. Only two people know if he raped your mother or if they were in love—Thomas and Hannah. Only Thomas is alive to tell the story. You will either believe him, or you will not."

"Why would my mother's people say it was rape if it wasn't?"

"To save themselves from disappointment in your mother, or to save you from the Anointed," I speculate. "It would have probably been easier to have them accept you if your mother was a victim."

Rachel is silent for several moments.

"Shall we continue?" Breanne asks.

Rachel nods, and Breanne calls Thomas back over to us.

"I will accept your claim of parentage, without going to Grover for the test, but I am still not sure if I can trust you," Rachel says. "That may take a while."

"I will give you all the time you need," Thomas says. He moves as if to get closer to her, then hesitates before stepping back. He glances at Gotham when he approaches.

"It's been a long day," Gotham says. "Why don't we call it a night? Further plans can be made tomorrow when we are all fresh."

"I agree," Breanne says. She turns to Lewis. "You will sleep with your contingent tonight. Thomas will stay on the east side of camp with my people."

I know she is keeping Thomas from any chance to collude with Lewis, or get too close to Rachel. I am not certain I will be able to sleep—I may try to keep one eye open to make sure no one but me gets near Rachel. I don't fear Thomas, but I don't yet trust him either.

Rachel and I go to our bedding and press our bodies as close as we can get them under the light blanket. Things have changed in our camp and I hope it is for the better—but am sure we won't really know until the morning greets us.

"Good night, love," I whisper.

She clutches me to her. "Good night."

CHAPTER ELEVEN

Rachel and I sit with my three siblings, Thomas, Aaron, and half a dozen of our warriors. We settle apart from the rest of the group to be out of the constant din of voices. We number over a hundred now.

Thomas clears his throat before speaking.

"I know who among my people desires peace. And I know who will be loyal to General Grayson and General Brodie to the bitter end. Luckily, the latter are few."

"Tell us about General Grayson," Breanne says.

"My father's health is in decline. A replacement to lead his people has not yet been named, which will work in our favor."

"How will we separate those loyal to the Resistance Army among your people from the ones we can trust?" Gotham asks.

"I can send the questionable ones on a false mission to get them away from the technology. I don't wish them harm, but they cannot be trusted with our secrets. When they are on their journey in the other direction, those who desire peace will join us along with the technology at hand, and swell the ranks of your Peace Movement."

"But then your people loyal to the Generals will still be out there, and still be a liability," Breanne states. "We cannot take any chances."

"We understand that you don't want harm to come to any of your people. But we can't risk them coming after us later," Gotham adds.

Thomas nods, appears pensive as he stares into the fire.

"You propose we take them prisoner?" he asks, his voice strained.

"Surely you understand that for peace to be truly acquired we must be totally committed?" Breanne asks.

Thomas nods. "What do you suggest?"

"You send the Resistance-loyal people across the river with orders to wait for you. Once they are on this side and separated from the others, you come back across to them and lead their surrender."

His nostrils flare.

"Are you with us Sergeant?" Breanne asks, her voice bordering on icy.

He breathes deeply and glances toward Rachel. Then he turns back to Breanne.

"I am with you."

"When they arrive on this side of the river they will be surrounded. We will take them peacefully if you can facilitate that, or by force, if they do not cooperate. If you are to convince them to surrender, you will need to give them the speech of your life." Breanne stares at him for a long time. "And you will also need to give the ones you believe to be on our side a convincing, unifying speech."

I wonder if Thomas has the same relationship with his people that Breanne has with hers. She gives passionate, rousing orations when she needs to.

"Lewis," Breanne says, turning to our brother. "Your mission will be to accompany Thomas across the river and back again. Do a good job and your wife and baby can join you back in Lutherville after we have won our peace."

Lewis nods his head and I'm convinced he believes the barely veiled threat against his family is real. I can't imagine that Breanne would hurt Cora and Daphne, but I really don't want to find out for sure.

"Kai, you and Stevens are familiar with Ellenton. You two take a dozen others—all from Stevens' territories—with you and go into the heart of the city, where the remains of the bridge are, and take up strategic positions." She waits until I nod my agreement, then goes on. "Bring your bow and the gun. You are in charge of your group, and Stevens is your second."

I see Rachel watching Breanne closely, almost as if she's willing my sister to give her permission to go with us into Ellenton.

For a second, it appears Breanne is considering it.

"Rachel, I want you to stay here and keep an eye on Cora and the baby." Breanne glances at Lewis. "You will continue to treat Cora as a guest as long as she acts like one. Keep your bow handy and protect Lewis's family while we are gone."

Rachel nods. I wonder if she feels like she's moved back in time, being asked to play guard to them.

"I understand my mission," Rachel says.

Breanne gives her a look that resembles affection mixed with respect.

"Myself, Gotham, Shelton, and Nell, we'll take our contingents to the edge of the city and wait there. Everyone else protects the perimeter of our camp. Any questions?" Breanne waits only a moment for a response, then says, "Good. Everyone stay vigilant and safe."

†

It is slow going as we pick our way through the rubble that is Ellenton. Stevens and I position ourselves on opposite ends of a wall that appears to once have belonged to a school. I've never been to a real school, but I believe the rows of small desks are a good indicator.

We wait for a long time, fourteen of us in all, strategically placed in a semicircle near the remains of the bridge I'd crossed with Thomas and Aaron. The water is still deep and black, but lacks the momentum that gave it the roaring presence it had the last time I saw it.

For a second I believe I am remembering the sound of the thundering water, but then I realize it is the sound of motorbikes crossing the bridge. I watch as one by one the dirty, loud motorbikes jump the crumbling expanse of concrete and then drive down the side and halt just ten or fifteen feet from where we are hiding behind the partial wall.

There are nine soldiers, including Aaron, who stop and turn off their engines. When I peek around the edge of the wall, I recognize one of them as a man whom I had met at the end of his rifle when I'd first crossed over to meet Thomas. Aaron is taking off his backpack, looking quite relaxed, and unlike someone who is about to help facilitate the surrender of his fellow soldiers. For a moment I worry that perhaps he isn't so much on the side of peace after all.

Aaron has gathered the others off to the side, bringing them in closely with an offering of cigarettes. Only a few take them. They all look up at the sound of another motorbike crossing the river. I lift my head just enough to confirm that it is Thomas.

When Thomas dismounts his machine the soldiers salute him. It has been so easy, while watching him look adoringly across the fire at Rachel, to forget that he is a Sergeant in the Resistance Army. Well, will be for only a few more minutes. Once he turns on his men, he will become Peace Warrior instead of Army Sergeant.

"Where are the other soldiers we were to meet?" someone asks.

"And why are we here without our rifles?"

"Place all packs in the middle of this clearing," Thomas says.

"What is this all about?"

"Are you disobeying a direct order?" Thomas yells.

"No, sir." The soldier does as he's told, and the others follow suit.

"I have chosen you—each one of you—because I am convinced beyond a doubt of your loyalty to the Resistance Army."

The men all pound their chests and yell, "Resist!"

Bile burns the base of my throat.

"Because of that loyalty, I must now ask you to lay down your arms—all of your arms. Handguns as well." There is a lot of grumbling, but all seem to comply.

"Looks too much like an easy ambush," one of the men says. All eyes turn to that man, except mine, mine are locked onto a soldier at the other end of the semicircle. I watch as that man starts inching along the row of motorbikes.

Aaron, his gun still held in front of him, is at the end closest to the man who is obviously up to something. But Aaron is also looking at the man who just spoke and doesn't seem to notice the other one, closer to him, reaching for something in the back of his waistband.

"Do not question my leadership," Thomas says, seemingly oblivious to the tension that is building. Or is he?

When the man reaches for something behind his back, I fire a warning arrow that embeds in the seat of the motorbike just inches from him. He freezes. Then he slowly puts his hands up. Aaron moves behind him and confiscates the handgun he'd been reaching for.

"Anyone else?" Thomas asks.

I only hear snippets of what Thomas says over the roaring of blood in my ears. I hope my hands do not begin to sweat.

The soldiers are looking around, nervously, eying their weapons on the ground. We still have the soldiers off balance, but I know that diminishes with every second that passes. I make the decision and show myself, then Stevens follows my lead. Within seconds, all fourteen of us are standing in full view, arrows nocked on our bows, pointed at the soldiers.

"The next one won't be a warning shot," I call out when one soldier takes a tentative step toward the weapons.

The man steps back.

"I want to see everyone's hands." Thomas lifts his rifle into firing position. "Anyone who doesn't comply will be wearing an arrow in their chest. Do you understand?"

No one answers.

"I said, do you understand!" Thomas shouts, sounding to me like a Sergeant for the first time since I met him.

"Yes, sir," one man says as he puts his hands on the top of his head and goes down to his knees.

One by one, the soldiers relent. Aaron binds their hands behind their backs as Thomas keeps his gun at the ready, and the rest of us keep our bows in firing position.

I hear the sound of another motorbike and hope that it is Lewis. Until he comes to a complete stop and dismounts, I keep my arrow aimed at his chest. He turns, looks at me and winks. I smile as I lower my bow.

We leave the motorbikes behind and lead the prisoners along the edge of the river. It is safer that way than to pick our way through the rubble with them. It takes much longer, but it is an easier option. When we get to the edge of the city, we are met by at least a hundred warriors, most on horseback.

Back at camp, it is decided that we will keep the motorbikes in Ellenton until we have a need for them. The prisoners will be escorted in the morning to McNally.

I am settled in front of the fire with Rachel at my side. I smile as I look across camp and see Lewis embrace his wife and child.

CHAPTER TWELVE

We are camped between Karst and my family home. It feels strange to have come back this way, to be so close to Karst and not be able to go there yet.

"You and Rachel are to lead the group going to ND3 to liberate it from the Resistance Army. We will all stay with you until you are just southeast of Mt. Sanders, then we will go west and you will continue south to ND3 with your people," Breanne says.

"That is not a real mission. I want to go with you and Gotham, I want to fight beside you." I cross my arms over my chest and stare at my sister.

"No. Your mission is to use your diverse knowledge of ND3 to determine who is friend and who is foe, who is worthy of joining the Peace Movement, and who needs further scrutiny." Breanne places her hand on my arm. "It's an honorable mission, Kai. No one can do this as well as you and Rachel."

"But I am a warrior." I feel like a petulant child but cannot help myself.

"Yes, you are. And it will take a warrior to accomplish this." She squeezes my shoulder. "I am giving you the responsibility of going to ND3 and classifying everyone there as you see necessary. You and Rachel know the facility from a unique perspective, and that is invaluable to us. We will rely on your judgment as to whether or not someone should be trusted. You must determine who of the guards and prisoners should be granted freedom, who is a danger to us and should be incarcerated, and who lies somewhere in the middle of the spectrum."

I glance at Rachel and she is nodding her head to Breanne's words. I hope she does believe the words themselves and is not just caught up in the power Breanne uses to effectively communicate her will.

"But—" I start to argue.

"Are you questioning my leadership?"

I am surprised Breanne would ask me this in front of Rachel. I am ashamed that she feels it necessary. "No, I'm not. I just don't want to be coddled."

"On the contrary," Breanne says, her voice gentle. "I am giving you and Rachel a pivotal job for the movement. Now, won't you accept the mission and go to ND3 and make me proud—no *prouder*?"

I look at Rachel, then back to Breanne.

"Yes. I accept the mission. Count me in."

"Rachel?" Breanne asks.

"Count on me as well."

Later, I ask Rachel how she feels about returning to ND3.

She rakes her teeth against her lower lip before speaking.

"I feel a bit overwhelmed at the prospect, but know it is an honorable mission and we must do it."

"My brave girl," I whisper into her neck as I pull her against me. "We will go to ND3 and get our closure—physically and emotionally." It is then that I truly appreciate the gift that Breanne is giving us.

Breanne calls all the original members of our contingent of the Peace Movement warriors to her. She calls out names of those who will break out into smaller groups to take leave of the main fighting group.

Carlos and Nell are going with a group to ND2, then to two nearby Employment Centers. Shelton is going with a small group to Thomas's settlement to help guard the technology. Rachel and I are assigned twenty people, including Patricia, to go to ND3.

"Will twenty-two people be enough?" I ask Breanne.

"Yes." She nods. "Our intel is that there are fewer than one hundred prisoners at ND3 now."

I ponder that. There were close to four hundred during my incarceration.

"And how many guards?"

"That we are unsure of," Breanne answers.

I nod, placing my trust in my sister's intel *and* judgement.

All of us in liberating contingents are to leave early the following day.

Rachel and I go to a stump off to the side and eat a dinner of mostly mixed grain mush and stale bread, with a little rabbit. I normally do not eat animal protein other than eggs and cheese, but something in my body is telling me I need more protein, more than ever since our cheese and vegetables are now all consumed or rotten beyond use. I will listen to my body.

After we eat, we examine and pack the supplies we will need for the journey back to ND3. It will take us three days if the weather stays the same, four or five if the storms that have been building to the north and west make it to us before we are at our destination. As much as I look forward to the relief the rain brings from the persistent heat, too much of it will flood the dry riverbeds, making travel more difficult, just as it was with the Black River.

While we are packing our supplies, Thomas approaches.

"Good luck on your mission. Please stay safe."

"Thank you." Rachel's body language still shows her doubt, but she is sweet and shy around her father. "And your mission? Where are you headed?"

"I will be going after General Grayson's contingent."

I raise an eyebrow at the thought that he will be sent after his own flesh and blood.

"I believe my father is incapacitated. Chances are he's in a medical facility already." He looks down at the ground, then looks up at Rachel. "I was wondering—hoping, actually—that I could embrace you once before we prepare to take our leave?"

Rachel takes a tentative step forward, then steps awkwardly into his arms. Her back is to me, but I see the relief etched onto Thomas's face. When she steps away, he looks at me.

"I am glad Rachel will be with you, Kai. Keep my daughter safe, please."

"Of course," I say, trying to figure out how I feel about his words of possession toward my lover. "You be safe as well."

†

It is not an accident that we arrive at ND3 before dawn on a Saturday. Although many in the Resistance are not spiritual, they still often partake in the Friday night purge, when they all drink shine until they can imbibe no more. Saturday mornings are full of headaches and queasy stomachs to go with incantations and incense.

I dismount Shakespeare when we are fifty or so yards from the complex. Rachel looks at me in the way that I know she means for me to be careful. I give her a slight nod. I am to take five others with me, go in stealthily, and assess the guard situation.

We approach unencumbered. There is an unnatural stillness, a haunted feeling that gives me gooseflesh on my arms. I have just opened the door, looked in, and entered when I hear a noise to my right.

I lift my handgun up into position to shoot.

"Easy there, Inmate 8895. Or should I say, Kai Brodie?" Maria smiles at me as she steps out of the shadows. Her pants are too short for her long legs, a detail that makes me smile.

"Ah, Maria," I say.

"When I found out after the liberation that you were a Brodie, things began to make more sense." She nods at my gun. "Relax, there is only myself and Tara up and about. You remember Tara?"

Another woman steps out of the shadows. It is the woman who had saved me from slipping in the shower, the woman whose name I'd never learned.

"The guards are in their quarters, the inmates in their cells," Tara says in a low voice.

I nod. "Let's move then."

We slowly and silently begin blocking the interior exit doors to the guards' quarters. Once done, I step back outside and let out a coywolf yelp. Within minutes the sound of hoof beats are in the air. I go inside and rejoin Maria and Tara while some of the others remain outside to guard the exterior doors from the guards' quarters.

"Let's start on the east side and move methodically toward the west. You five come with me." I gesture towards the original group that came in with me. "And Rachel, you are with us as well. We need to inventory the people first," I stop in the middle of my sentence when I realize how cold that sounds. "We must *assess* everyone first, take care of basic needs, then start sorting."

I step into the main corridor and the smell assails me. Someone stands close enough behind me that I feel the heat from their body, and when I glance over my shoulder I see it is Rachel. The look on her face tells me the smell has registered with her as well. It reeks of unclean toilets and…and death.

When I approach the first cell, my breath leaves me and I want to vomit. The women's faces peering back at me are so gaunt they almost don't look human. Rachel's gasp draws my attention back to her. She has her hand over her mouth and nose and tears are running down her face.

I look at Maria, and I am about to verbally lash out at her.

"Tara and I just transferred in two days ago. We were as appalled as you are."

"Rachel, please radio Dunn that we need a doctor in here now. And then radio command—we need all the medical personnel they can send."

She's on the radio within seconds, looking like she's glad for something to do, but like she still might be sick.

We continue down the corridor, stopping just long enough at the barred doors of each cell to get an idea of the inmates' conditions. My eyes are watering and I'm not sure if it's from the stench or my breaking heart.

As we turn the corner and go down the next corridor, we notice this one houses men. They too look like they've not been out or fed in a long time. This isn't a detention center, it's a death camp. As horrible as my incarceration had been, I cannot imagine the hell these people have been through. What was the Resistance trying to do, starve them all to death?

My eyes scan the occupants of one cell, causing me to stop short. I immediately recognize the man with the scar on his face as he looks up at me from his prone position on the floor.

"The doctor's here," Rachel says from behind me. "Where shall she begin?"

"She can begin here." I look behind Rachel to where Tara stands. "Unlock this cell door, please."

Tara nods and moves forward to do so.

"Cooper?" Rachel whispers from behind me.

"Would you like to stay with Doc to help her here?" I ask Rachel.

"Whatever you wish of me," she says.

"Stay if you are able."

"Kai," Maria says as she rushes up behind me. "Brandon needs you. The guards are getting more and more hostile. They're trying to break through the barrier."

I give Rachel one more glance, see her assisting Doc, and follow Maria back down the corridor.

Brandon is pacing in front of the barricaded door to the guard's quarters. "This could get ugly."

"Nothing can be as ugly as what I just saw." I step up closer to the window high on the door and form my hands around my mouth to try to amplify the sound. "Let me have your attention! We are the warriors for the Peace Movement. The Resistance's control of ND3 ends now."

"Go to hell!" someone yells from the other side of the barricade.

"Over my dead body," someone else chimes in.

"As you wish!" I turn to Brandon. "Anyone with even the slightest amount of medical training is to help with the inmates. All others are to be heavily armed and with me here. Maria!"

"I am right here," she says.

"Do they have arms in the quarters?"

"As we were previously instructed, we swept through during the night and took up whatever arms we could see. There might be a few that were too well hidden."

"How many guards total are there?"

"Ten."

"What?" That is only a fraction of the number of guards from when I was imprisoned here.

"It's not like the inmates are in any condition to do anything."

"Are there any guards here that you feel might be Peace Movement material?" I ask.

"Everyone in there has been here for six months or longer. Whether they participated in this disgusting situation or just did nothing while things got this bad, they are guilty of heinous behavior." She holds my gaze. "It will not hurt my feelings if we simply gas the guards in there as they are. Too bad we don't have any gas with us."

I'm thinking she might be right, but that wasn't my instruction. "The outside perimeter is still secured?"

"Yes," Brandon says.

"If anyone tries to escape through windows or any other way, they are to be captured or shot on the spot, whichever is safest for our people." I turn to face the remaining people under my command. "We are going to invite them to come out through this interior door. Anyone who doesn't cooperate and come out with their hands empty and visible can be dealt with as harshly as necessary, up to and including death."

"Yes, ma'am," several say.

I position my hands around my mouth again. "We are unblocking the door. Come out in an orderly fashion with your hands on your head. Please do not make us hurt you."

"Remove the barricade," I say to Brandon and another man.

Each Peace warrior has a bow, knife, or gun at the ready. The guards do not come at first.

"Shall we shoot blindly into your corridor and quarters?" I ask.

"I am unarmed." A man comes out with his hands in the air.

The warrior to my left takes the guard down to his knees and binds his hands behind his back.

Two more guards come out and are taken down in the same fashion. The fourth person through the door stops abruptly when she sees me. My finger twitches on the trigger of my gun. I silently dare Leona to make a wrong move.

"Well, well, I really am seein' Artemis," she says, hatred dripping from her words. "I shouldn't be surprised."

"Hands up," I remind her. I am not going to respond to her barb. I know I will resist the temptation to harm her because I will never abuse power in the ways she has. I want her alive and well when she is incarcerated for the heinous crimes that have been perpetrated against these people.

Leona does as she's told and Brandon brings her down to the ground. My attention goes back to the advancing guards. All goes well until the final one. He charges at me, but is shot by Brandon, who has to release Leona without adequately binding her.

In just seconds Leona is on me. My gun is knocked free and she pulls me to her to use as a shield against all the weapons that are now trained on her.

"Go ahead and fill 'er with holes." She tightens the grip she has on my neck from behind me. I know how strong this woman is, and fear she could snap my neck without any difficulty.

The closest warriors take a few steps back.

Her arm presses into my throat, crushing against my windpipe. I look toward the door just as Rachel comes out of the corridor. Rachel's expression begins to crumble.

"Holy shit, I'm seein' the guard we all wanted to bed down with." Leona has recognized Rachel. She laughs. "You turned the sexy guard into one of you?"

I know with her focus on Rachel it is the time to act. I hold onto the arm choking me with one hand and reach for the knife strapped to my calf with the other. Before she can react, I am swinging upward and sinking the blade into her neck.

She is clutching at her wound, gasping and choking, and we all stare numbly at her. After several quiet moments, I grab a rag Rachel holds out to me and attempt to apply pressure to the wound. I know the cut is a mortal one, but feel I should offer the ease of letting her think we care enough to try to save her. It is fruitless and she is soon lifeless.

I leave Leona's body propped up against the wall and begin helping my comrades assist the near-death inmates. All together, we find a dozen decomposing bodies, twenty-five souls on the verge of leaving this earth, and another seventy-one in need of medical care but not too far gone to be saved.

We keep tending them long after the additional medical personnel have arrived. We set up caravans of injured to be treated at a makeshift hospital until they can be transported to the facility in Grover.

Supplies and gear are pilfered from the complex. Once everyone has been removed from inside, we burn ND3 to the ground, just as other Peace Movement groups are doing to the NDs and ECs all across New America. Only the prison in McNally, one on the northern border, and two along the western edge of New America will be left intact for criminals and those who will oppose peace.

†

Rachel rides on Shakespeare with me so that Maria and Tara can double up on the horse Rachel rode to ND3. We have all been quiet on our return trip. Rachel rests her head against my back and I know she is exhausted and devastated by what we witnessed at the prison.

I had no problem focusing while working to save the inmates, but now that the adrenaline has worn off, I have a lump in my throat that feels like a boulder. I fight tears as I think of how Rachel could have been one of those inmates. Had she not gotten out… No, I cannot think about that now.

We are within an hour of returning to base camp when the hair on the back of my neck stands on end. Ajax sprints to meet us and runs in a panicked circle around our group. The coywolf yowls and holds eye contact with me as he does.

Something is seriously wrong. Rachel knows this as well, as demonstrated by how hard she grips me around my waist.

We hear the sounds of fighting before we see the bloody scene around the bend. Shakespeare rears up on his hind legs and snorts loudly. It feels like a battle cry.

We ride closer to the fighting and I can feel Rachel moving behind me on the horse. I see in my peripheral vision that she has readied her bow.

"You get us there, I'll take what shots I can," she says.

I squeeze Shakespeare tighter with my legs and lean toward his muscular neck. He bolts forward. Ajax is running alongside us. When we near, the Army's horses grow even more uneasy, but ours are familiar with the coywolf and stay steady.

There are casualties on both sides. Many of our downed warriors appear to have been shot, but most of the army soldiers are wielding swords or trying to use their guns as clubs now. Perhaps they've run out of bullets?

Ajax flies at a soldier about to bludgeon a peace warrior, knocking him off his horse. I am amazed that the animal was able to get the height needed to take down the soldier. Ajax has him stunned and pinned in just moments, but gets up when one of our warriors gives a coywolf yelp. As soon as Ajax is out of the line of fire, the warrior shoots an arrow into the neck of the soldier, stopping him cold.

My attention goes to Shawn, who is in a fierce swordfight with a soldier. Just when I think he will be taken down, one of Rachel's arrows strikes his opponent in the thigh. When he reaches for the source of the pain, Shawn finishes him off. I glance behind me to see Rachel's reaction to what she's done and there is only serious concentration on her face as she readies the next arrow.

Shakespeare spins around and I see Stevens is in trouble, fighting two soldiers. I steer the horse toward them as I grab the knife strapped to my leg. I pull up short and throw the knife, hitting one soldier in the gut just as Rachel finds her target with the other's chest.

We are too evenly matched for this to not end in disaster. I am looking around frantically for my siblings when to the east there is a cloud of dust. The silhouettes that emerge are of a vast number of warriors on horseback, creating a thunderous roar as they near us. A high-pitched war cry rings out and I hear Breanne answer it with one of her own. Our people are energized by the addition of the eighty or so warriors.

Rachel pulls back on her bowstring and an arrow hits its mark, saving Lewis from a sword. She still doesn't react to what she's done as she readies to draw back again. I see Jonas at the same moment he locks his eyes onto me. He rides hard, in our direction. Just when I think he will knock us both off the horse, Rachel takes the shot. His horse just skims ours, not causing any damage, and Jonas falls to the ground.

I ride over and he looks up at me with lifeless eyes. I think how his eyes aren't any more soulless dead as they were alive.

I feel the tremble in Rachel's fingers as she grips my side. I am contemplating how she will deal with having a hand in these deaths, but I am distracted when Gotham lets out a primal roar before sinking his sword deep into a soldier.

Shakespeare high-steps and dances around, unsure what to do until I pull in on the reins and halt him. When he settles down I glance around and see that all of the Resistance Army has been neutralized, either killed or taken prisoner.

I am shocked when I see Father sprawled on the ground, about five feet from the tip of Breanne's sword.

"Surrender, General," Breanne says, her voice cold and measured.

"Never," Father says through clenched teeth, his square jaw not moving with the word. He gets up onto his knees, turns away from Breanne and looks at me. "I should have gutted you when I had you strung up like an animal."

I stare at him, speechless. A mix of sadness and anger races through me and the only thought I can form is that this man was always a General first, a father last.

General Brodie springs forward, rushing at me with a knife, but Lewis steps in front of Breanne, and between Father and me, and buries a sword into Father's stomach.

The general is lifeless, on the ground, the knife he'd tried to stab me with in the dirt beside him.

I dismount Shakespeare and run to my brother.

"Lewis," I say, reaching for him.

He steps away from me.

"Please. I'd like to be alone," he whispers, then he begins walking toward the tree line.

That is when I hear Sebastian's voice. "Traitors! Burn in hell, all of you!"

Breanne nods at Shawn and he leads my nephew to the holding area for the prisoners.

"What will come of Sebastian now?" I ask.

"We will hold him somewhere safe, somewhere he can be monitored. If we are lucky, he will see that we only did what we had to do, and he will not only forgive us, but join us."

"And if he doesn't?"

"We will take extra care with him, do not worry." She walks away, leaving her words to calm me.

There is a shout, then the wild-haired warrior who led the reinforcements to join with us during our weakest moment is embracing Breanne. When they step away from one another, the beautiful warrior looks around. The ground all about us is littered with bodies.

"You throw one hell of a party," the woman says.

"And you are one hell of a guest of honor." Breanne looks around then until her sight settles on me. She comes to me, takes my hand, and leads me over. "Naomi, let me introduce you to my sister, Kai Brodie, Peace Warrior."

"It is wonderful to finally meet you." Naomi smiles and holds out her hand. She takes my hand in hers.

"And this is Rachel, Kai's partner." My sister gestures Rachel over to us.

"Rachel," Naomi says with a smile. "Ah, ha."

Breanne elbows Naomi as Gotham heads our way. The smile that passes between the two women is playful. I wonder if they will share the joke with me one day.

"Are you sure you are all right?" I take Rachel's hand and lead her away from the others.

She smiles, a bittersweet expression that doesn't quite reach her eyes. "I am fine."

"You would tell me if you weren't?" I ask.

She kisses my forehead and appears to relax a little. "I would tell you," she says, and my heart sings with my belief in her.

†

Later that day, I look across the fire at Breanne and Gotham and my chest fills with pride. The twins have always been precious to me, but now—now I am thrilled to share them with the world.

Rachel squeezes my leg in a way that makes me think she can read the pride on my face. I smile at her and my chest fills even more. How did I get so blessed? I bring Rachel's hand to my face and kiss her palm.

I look over to my right when Lewis walks in our direction from the trees where he has been hunting peace for what he has done to Father. He sits beside me.

"Are you okay?" I ask.

"Yes, Kai, I am."

"You saved my life."

"And I would do it a hundred times more."

Someone somewhere plays a flute. The music and the fire blend together in such a dynamic way. I glance over to where Gotham watches Breanne, Shawn, and Naomi. He is staring at Naomi with so much adoration that it makes me feel uneasy. The way she only partly acknowledges him tells me he will have his heart broken if he's not careful.

My attention leaves them as Breanne circles the fire and sits between me and Lewis.

"I am fine, Breanne." He beats her to her inquiry.

"I know." She puts her hand on his shoulder for a brief moment, then turns to me. "Your next mission is to escort Camryn to Karst. She will be here early tomorrow."

Rachel squeezes my hand and Breanne laughs.

"And your next mission, Rachel, is to make sure Kai gets her mission accomplished without getting into any trouble." Breanne smiles. "Do you accept your mission?"

"Yes, I accept," Rachel says.

Breanne gestures toward the outermost part of our camp where Shawn is giving a bowl of water to Ajax.

"You do know that Shawn wants Ajax to stay with us when you leave for Karst?"

"And you do know that will be totally up to Ajax, right?" I tease.

Rachel laughs, then her attention goes somewhere across camp. I see that Thomas is making his way toward us. When he is within a few feet, Rachel stands. He hesitates for only a moment before embracing her. He lets her go and approaches me.

"Thomas, your mission went well?" I ask.

"Yes, it did. We easily overcame my father's soldiers."

"And the General?"

"He is very ill, at a medical facility, under guard, but will not be with us on this earth for much longer." He places a hand on each of my shoulders. "I have heard of the conditions at ND3 and some of the other prisons. If you had not gotten Rachel out with you—" He sobs, then pulls me into an embrace. I allow him to do so as I fight my own tears.

When he releases his hold on me we all sit together. Across the fire several of our warriors are celebrating our victory with some shine. I look at Breanne to see her reaction and she shrugs at me.

"Let them have their fun. Things will be serious enough again in no time."

"What's next?" I ask her.

"Now that our warriors have joined with Naomi's from the east, there is only Roger of the Northern territories for us to come together with."

"You know this Roger well?" I am still amazed by all that Breanne knows and all who are so dedicated to her.

"Yes, Roger is another key player, along with Naomi. We each had our mission to bring together the isolated populations of our territories with those ready for peace apart from both the Anointed and Resistance."

"The Resistance Army has been defeated, so what is left to do?" I ask.

"There are still small pockets of people who do not support peace, especially the Feral population. They will need to be dealt with, probably through force." Breanne leans forward, no longer as relaxed. "Then there is the matter of keeping the peace, which will need every ounce of diplomacy and decency we can find."

EPILOGUE

The heavy rains started just before we arrived at Karst. I am happy for the life the precipitation brings, and the relief from the heat it allows, but I am also filled with joy to be dry inside the cave network, standing before some of my tribe.

There is not time to think about the weather right now. Nor is there time to think of the approaching day when we will leave to go to the main Rehabilitation Center, where we will help women who have never known true freedom acclimate to this new world, full of possibilities. There is no time for those thoughts, for today is the day of our binding. Today Suzanna will bind mine and Rachel's hearts and souls together for eternity.

I only steal quick glances at Rachel for now because I need to be able to get through the ceremony without my legs turning into jelly and bringing me to my knees. When we approached one another at the altar moments ago, I had noticed how, even though her robe is identical to mine, it fits her in a manner that renders me breathless. I chuckle at myself, as I have been rendered breathless by her for the entire time I've known her.

Standing beside Rachel, I look around us. The love in the room is palpable.

Camryn's straight black hair falls into her face but doesn't hide that she has joyful tears in her eyes. I think back to the night before, when we embraced and let go of the negative memories, including those of my time in General Brodie's jail. I tell her I am grateful for the gift of life she bestowed on me when she helped me escape. She accepted my thanks and, as is customary, we will move on now, away from those memories.

My attention goes now to Heidi and Dawson, my elephant-soul and her rat. They hold hands as they return my smile. I understand this is their first time away from their baby boy, as he's been left with an aide for the duration of the ceremony. Heidi and Dawson are true friends and a shining example of love to be held up and admired.

Lewis and Cora stand beside them, also holding hands and smiling. I am so glad that Rachel and Cora have formed a deep friendship the last few days, joking together about the challenges of being coupled with a Brodie sibling. Lewis, Cora, and their daughter will be traveling with us to the Rehabilitation Center, and it will be nice to have some of our family there with us as we work for a healthy, peaceful future.

I wish Breanne, Gotham, and Thomas could be here with us, but understand their immense responsibilities. I know they are with us in spirit, and that we will see them again in due time.

"Shall we begin?" Suzanna asks.

I look at her and so many warm memories wash over me. At once I feel they are from both current days and previous lives. Suzanna must have been dreaming about me a lot lately for the lingering energy to be so strong. Light is playing off her flowing gray hair that makes me think of both a princess and an angel.

"Kai and Rachel," Suzanna begins.

I face my love—my very breath and life—and am almost overcome by the strong feelings of love and adoration I feel for her. Her light hair has grown in enough to be swept back away from her face. Her eyes are gold and amber, shining so beautifully my breath gets caught in my chest.

"I call upon the God and Goddess to bless the unity of Kai and Rachel—to wash them in the rays of sun and beams of moon—to lift up their love for the universe to kiss. God protect you, Goddess enlighten you, Universe bless you for the rest of your lives." She turns to face the others now. "May Kai and Rachel love always!"

"May they love always," the others echo.

"Kai, Rachel, do you vow to love and protect one another for all days."

"I vow to love and protect Rachel for all days," I say.

Rachel smiles. "I vow to love and protect Kai for all days."

Suzanna loops a silk cord around my neck and then around Rachel's. I feel energy flowing along the cord to encircle us both in perfect, peaceful warmth.

"To love always!" the room erupts.

I pull Rachel to me and hold her tight. I have waited my entire life to feel this connected, this completed. She pulls away just enough to press her lips against mine.

We are surrounded by shouts of joy. Everyone hugs and cries and I feel the love moving throughout the room, almost as if it is its own being.

The drink and laughter are still flowing easily when I take Rachel by the hand and sneak away to our temporary quarters. "Shouldn't we stay a little longer?" she asks.

"You aren't ready to join with me physically now that we have joined spiritually?" I tease.

The blush that runs up her pale neck to her cheeks tells me she is quite ready to join me in showing our love to one another's flesh.

"Yes," she says. "I am ready for just that."

We enter the quarters for bonded couples, acknowledge the private bathing facility, and find that someone has set up nearly a hundred candles. I cannot wait to see the light of the flames dance off Rachel's exquisite skin.

We slip off our flowing, silky marriage robes to expose our bare flesh. It is customary at Karst to not have too much clothing get in the way of consummating the binding of souls. My hands run down Rachel's sides and I pull her tight against me.

"Make love to me," she whispers.

I lower her onto the bedding and cover her with my heated body. My lips and hands are everywhere on her until I find the wetness between her legs and plunge my fingers inside her. I inhale her gasp, kiss her, and then whisper, "You are mine now."

She holds my gaze while she slips her hand between us. She strokes the length of my wetness until my body starts to tremble. "And you are mine."

Our bodies rock together, mingling our wetness into a frenzy of moans and half-screams, until our release draws out rapid, staccato breaths of love fully realized. Yes, I am hers now, and plan to be for not just this life but every single one after.

ABOUT THE AUTHOR

RENEE MACKENZIE

As a Navy brat, Renee MacKenzie lived on three continents before her family settled in Virginia. She currently resides in Naples, Florida with her partner and their poodle. Renee works for the National Park Service at Big Cypress National Preserve and enjoys Pickleball, wildlife photography, reading, and hiking. Even though Renee has been paid to do all sorts of jobs, ranging from dental assistant to bartender, field sampler to pet-sitter, and maintenance worker to property officer, she insists she's only had one job—writer—and all the rest has just been research.

Renee is the author of seven novels – *Confined Spaces*, *Flight*, *Nesting*, *23 Miles*, *Anywhere*, *Everywhere*, *Pausing*, and *Kai's Heart* (Book 1 in the Karst Series).

OTHER AFFINITY BOOKS

—————————————————————

<u>Free to Love</u> by Ali Spooner and Annette Mori
Captain Hillary Blythe loves sailing the ocean. Her journeys along the Atlantic Coast and Caribbean to deliver goods contain many adventures. When she brings a small group of rescued Africans to the Methodist mission on Antigua, challenges to deeply ingrained beliefs arise when she is drawn to one of the women—Kia.. Will Kia and Elizabeth be free to love among the harsh laws of the land and Elizabeth's struggles with her faith?

<u>Diamond Dreams</u> by Ali Spooner
Cameron St. Angelo dreams of playing softball in the College World Series. Earning a scholarship to play ball for her beloved LSU brings Cam one-step closer to achieving this dream. When Cam arrives on campus, she joins a family of women who share her love of the sport, and she realizes there is room in her life for another love.

<u>Unconventional Lovers</u> by Annette Mori
Bri and Siera are young women with huge hearts and strong wills; they want nothing more than to find a peaceful and secure space to be themselves. But the world is a harsh place for anyone who is different. Bri's Aunt Olivia is a vet who channels her emotions into her work and her love of Bri. Siera has her Aunt Deb who adores her. Despite their individual battles against hurt, prejudice and rejection, can these four women find love against the odds?

<u>Say You Won't Go</u> by JM Dragon & Erin O'Reilly
Logan Perry spent part of an inheritance traveling to various states, unconsciously looking for something to focus her life on. Taryn Donovan has no self-esteem and hates the waitressing job that barely keeps her in food. Can an unexpected weekend encounter turn out to be something more fulfilling? Find out in this sexually charged romance.

<u>Playing with Matches</u> by Lacey Schmidt
Dr. Augusta Stuart has devoted her adult life to supporting the mental health of disadvantaged children and moves to a new clinic in San Antonio. Her friend sets her up on a date with Callia Alexana. Prickly debates are somehow as unexpectedly fascinating as playing with matches, and Gus is forced to consider what preconceptions she is willing to burn to find true love.

<u>Changing Perspectives</u> by Jen Silver
Art director, Dani Barker, lives life on the edge and finance director Camila Callaghan thinks it's necessary to stay in the closet to maintain her position. When Dani and Camila meet,

they both sense an attraction, A change of perspective for both women is needed if they are to act on it.

Death is Only the Beginning by JM Dragon
What would you do if you were in a fatal accident with a stranger and ended up in heaven with them? Only to find out it wasn't an accident, it was murder. Follow the ghostly adventures of these two acrimonious strangers, who help two women find love and find closure for their predicament.

For the Love of a Woman by S. Anne Gardner
Enter a world where oil is supreme, passion rules reason and there is always the threat of civil war. In this jungle of power Raisa Andieta resides as one of its masters. Her only desire is to rule it alone. Carolyn Stenbeck is just trying to keep her marriage together. Her only desire is to be able to escape and never look back. When Raisa and Carolyn meet, it is like fuel and fire…a storm is brewing. Civil War is in the air, and passion like the coming storm begins to erupt.

The Bee Charmer by Ali Spooner
After the death of her father, Nat St. Croix needs to decide on which direction her life should take. Does she continue her life alone, as a trapper and trader, or does she start over and try to fit into a town surrounded by strangers? Will the call of the wild and all that is familiar win out, or will the call of love capture Nat's heart?

9 781988 549231